UNDER THE SUN

The Former Yugoslavia in 1993

Austria

Hungary

Balaton

Slovenia

Italy

★ Ljubljana

Zagreb ★

Croatia

Vojvodina
(autonomous province)

● Novi Sad

Romania

The Children's
Village

Bosnia and
Herzegovina

★ Belgrade

Serbia

Sarajevo ★

Montenegro

Pristina ●

Kosovo
(autonomous
province)

Bulgaria

Adriatic Sea

Podgorica ★

★ Skopje

Italy

Macedonia

Albania

Greece

0   100 Kilometers
0   100 Miles

UNDER THE SUN

Arthur Dorros

Amulet Books
New York

Design: Interrobang Design Studio
Map by: Rick Britton

Library of Congress Cataloging-in-Publication Data

Dorros, Arthur.
Under the sun / Arthur Dorros.
p. cm.
Summary: Chronicles the harrowing journey of Ehmet, a thirteen-year-old boy from Sarajevo who gets caught up in the ethnic conflicts in the former Yugoslavia.
ISBN 0-8109-4933-4
1. Yugoslav War, 1991-1995—Juvenile fiction. [1. Yugoslav War, 1991-1995—Fiction. 2. Bosnia and Herzegovina—History—1992—Fiction. 3. Prejudices—Fiction.] I. Title.

PZ7.D7294Un 2004
[Fic]—dc22
2004011183

Printed and bound in U.S.A.
10 9 8 7 6 5 4 3 2 1

AMULET

Published in 2004 by Amulet Books,
a division of Harry N. Abrams, Inc.
100 Fifth Avenue
New York, NY 10011
www.abramsbooks.com

Abrams is a subsidiary of
LA MARTINIÈRE
GROUPE

For those who dream

CONTENTS

UNDER THE SUN

ONE

◇

The Giant

Ehmet hung in the branches of the Giant. The sky was close at hand. Kids chased through the park below, laughing, trying to tag each other. A teenaged boy dribbled a basketball along the sidewalk, skillfully weaving around an old lady who pushed her two-wheeled metal cart heaped with clothes and topped by an ancient table lamp.

"Look, there's Darko," Ehmet whispered to his friend Milan, hidden in the treetop leaves nearby. A tall, big-framed boy had just entered the park, stopping to eye the old lady.

Milan loosed one hand from a branch and gave a thumbs-up to Ehmet. "Daaarko, Daaarko," Milan called out.

Darko spun, searching to see where the voice came from. The basketball and tag players had disappeared down a street, so the old lady methodically wheeling her cart was the only person visible in the park. Ehmet and Milan stayed quietly secreted in the treetop. Darko turned away to scan the surrounding sidewalks and lots filled with the rubble of what had been buildings.

"Daaarko, Daaarko," Ehmet called. Darko pivoted, trying to find the source of the sounds. He looked in the direction of the tree, though didn't think to look up. He kept his gaze at his own height.

When he turned away again, Milan and Ehmet called at him.

Darko ran around the park searching. He saw no one. "I'll get you," he shouted. He swung a leg with great force, kicking at an empty garbage barrel to demonstrate. He yelped, grabbed his foot and rubbed it, then hobbled out of the park.

It was all that Ehmet and Milan could do to keep from falling out of the tree with laughter. "That Darko," said Ehmet.

"Yeah, the Big Guy," added Milan. "He's still at least a head taller than anyone else in class. I mean, when there was a class."

"He could use an extra head," Ehmet said, "if he would think with it."

"Why think, if you can body block?" Milan asked.

Ehmet remembered the many times Darko had stopped him in the school hallways, saying "What have you got there?" and trying to go through his backpack. When he didn't find anything he liked, insults followed—"Stupid," "Blockhead," "Tail-dragger," and then, last year, "Muslim" and "Turk." Darko would brag that his family was "pure Croat."

"Pure jerk," Milan had said about Darko. "To him I'm 'The Serb.'"

"Come on, let's climb more," Ehmet suggested now.

The two climbed as high as possible, swaying in the treetop, watching the nearby clouds and surveying what they could see of the city. There was plenty of visibility; it was clear all around. The Giant was the last of what had once been a grand avenue of trees.

They watched two birds fly in with beaks streaming banners of grass and string. Ehmet found a nest the birds were building, held securely by the Giant's leafy arms. A blue and brown speckled egg sat like an island in the middle of its small, grassy sea.

"Look at this," said Milan. He picked a juicy, green caterpillar off a leaf to show Ehmet, and plopped it into a tattered, plastic bag he pulled from his pocket. Pushing leaves aside, Milan searched for other insects, but didn't find any. "Let's go look for more food for the chickens."

"Okay," said Ehmet, starting to descend the tree. "Last one down is a monkey's uncle."

"Serb, or Turk?" laughed Milan, mimicking Darko's name-calling. "No jumping."

They scrambled to the earth at the same time, both claiming to be there first, and raced across the park.

Huffing across the middle of a wide avenue, they ducked behind a large block of concrete that people called "Pink Floyd" because of the band's name that someone had painted on it. Ehmet and Milan had heard that some city workers had placed the block here one night, when it was safer to be outside. The piece of concrete appeared to be a friendly guardian. Ehmet and Milan were hiding, but not from Darko. "If you can see the snipers, they can see you," said Milan.

Ehmet and Milan peeked out from behind the block. Ehmet looked at the hills around Sarajevo that he had once seen as comforting blankets of green in summer or white in winter, but that now seemed to hold the city in a dangerous grip. Since the war had started last year, the Yugoslav army—now mostly Serb—and snipers had been firing down on the city from the hills. Other snipers—Muslim and Croat—had started firing into neighborhoods where they thought Serbs might live. No one knew exactly who was firing at any given moment. Whoever fired, it was nightmarish to walk anywhere these days.

"Found some new routes?" Milan asked. Ehmet and his friends exchanged tips on the safest routes with the kind of enthusiasm they had once used for sports news. A new route was a rare commodity, and highly valued until it proved unreliable. Each person had his or her favorite paths and ideas about them. Some people liked to use empty buildings and basements. Others felt that abandoned buildings might be dangerous, with their crumbling walls, unexpected company, or ammunition that had not exploded on impact. Ehmet generally preferred finding pathways between buildings.

"I think this way is good." Ehmet led Milan off the avenue, down a street lined with what Ehmet thought looked like dark carcasses of giant, metal beetles whose ribbed underbellies were turned to the sky. These were burned out buses, trucks, and cars that shells or rockets had hit. Vehicles that had carried people now helped shield their former passengers. Ehmet and Milan ducked behind the beetles when they felt too exposed to the hills.

"There's a bus!" said Milan as one passed at a distant intersection. They ran to catch it, but by the time they got to the intersection the bus was gone, and there was no other traffic in sight. Of the dozens of buses that used to run in the city, only a few still did from time to time. The drivers did their best to keep the surviving buses going, scrounging parts and fuel from anywhere they could. And more than once Ehmet had heard drivers tell passengers without enough money for the fare that they could ride anyway. Some of the buses used to take people out of the city, too. But no buses could leave the city now without being shot at. One bus that tried to leave was destroyed with over a hundred people—several that Ehmet knew—inside it.

They kept walking. Ehmet could feel the strength in his legs building from all the walking he'd been doing. He led them on a shortcut between buildings to cross to the next block.

"Oh, I see. There's your café. You just want to get some hot sauce, right?" Milan said.

"No, only a few bugs for the chickens. All that's eating here now is the insects." Ehmet plucked a shiny, brown, oval creature from a broken, metal table. He dropped the insect into the plastic bag Milan was holding open.

Ehmet and Milan both knew the café had been closed for months. With the roads not passable and even the airport closed, little went out of Sarajevo or came in. Food was priced as a precious luxury, and there was little food available, not enough to keep this café open. But before the war, Milan and Ehmet had often stopped here after school.

"Remember, Hot Pepper, remember?" Milan joked.

Ehmet remembered. He had spooned up half a bowl of hot sauce set on a table to spice the food, and swallowed the fiery goop. His friends had laughed and cheered him. They always teased him about how much he liked hot foods.

The waitress at the café, only a little older than Ehmet's thirteen years, had not been impressed. "You're crazy," she had told him. "If it doesn't hurt much today, it will tomorrow when you feel it on the other end." Ehmet was almost certain he wasn't crazy, though she had been right about the next day. He hadn't done that again. But he still liked hot sauce, even though it wasn't on his menu these days.

The trip to or from school had become nonexistent, too, after the building had been shelled.

Now it took other reasons to get out of the house. Getting food was one. Yet even shopping was dangerous these days.

Recently, Ehmet's mother had made her way to a back street near the Old City and found someone who was selling a few eggs, displayed on a cloth like jewels. She bought all six eggs for the going rate of ten American dollars each, a big dent in the family savings, but this was to be a special dinner—they had invited Milan's family to join them. The seller had packed the eggs carefully in a plastic bag. As Ehmet's mother walked home across a river bridge, a sniper fired. The bullet went through the plastic bag. Orange yolks and clear goo dripped out. All of the eggs were broken. Ehmet's mother was so angry at having lost the eggs that she arrived home without having stopped to think about the bullet missing her. It wasn't until a neighbor pointed out that she was fine that she laughed at herself for being more concerned about the eggs.

Milan's family had decided to have their own source of eggs, and traded their stereo system and a fashionable winter coat for three fluffy chicks. Since the family lived in an apartment five stories up, they had built a cage for the chicks on their terrace. Milan and Ehmet gathered insects for the growing chickens to eat.

The two clambered over a crumbled wall into what had been the yard of a house. Among what little sprouted in this rubble-strewn patch, Ehmet, who knew a lot about plants, had found edible ones. Now the place had been picked clean. Not a blade of grass remained.

"I don't know, whoever's been here took the stuff that's not edible, too," said Ehmet.

"Maybe there's nothing left for the bugs to eat either," said Milan, poking around the debris but turning up no insects.

"Or they're all leaving," Ehmet said. "Some of the ones that don't have a thousand legs can fly."

"We'd better fly, too," said Milan.

"Yeah," said Ehmet. "I've been gone a long time getting water." That was what he had talked to his mother about and how he had gotten out of the house, to go fill water jugs at one of the few working faucets in the city.

Milan took off toward his apartment, and Ehmet headed home. After a few blocks he stepped into the doorway of a fire-blackened building, felt in a dark corner, and retrieved two large plastic jugs.

He ran with the jugs for a few more blocks, and joined a line to wait his turn. People looked nervously at the hills. No one Ehmet knew well was here today. He filled the jugs and slung them on his shoulders.

"Water man!" Ehmet's mother said when he arrived home. She smiled, said it affectionately, with appreciation for his help and in an effort to lighten the situation. Yet it reminded Ehmet of how strange and difficult their lives had become. Everyday things that Ehmet hadn't thought much about before, things that had come with the touch of a button or the twist of a handle, like electricity and water, no longer came. At first his mother hadn't wanted Ehmet to be the one to go for water, but he had insisted. "I can't lock you in here," his mother had said.

The next day, Milan showed up at Ehmet's apartment, panting. "They're gone," he said. "They're gone!"

"Who?" Ehmet's mother asked.

"The chickens! I went to check them like I do every morning, and they were just gone!"

"How?" Ehmet asked.

"That's what we can't figure out. The cage was closed when I got there. Someone dropped on ropes . . . "

"Or used a helicopter?" Ehmet joked. It was difficult to imagine how someone had gotten onto the terrace that jutted out five stories above ground.

"No noise, no helicopter. It's weird."

"Desperation inspires some bizarre acts. Sorry that happened," said Ehmet's mother as she left the room.

"I heard on the way over here that they're cutting it," Milan said to Ehmet when his mother was out of hearing range.

"Cutting what?"

"The Giant."

The two of them had wondered when that might happen. With no heat, or other fuel, people gathered whatever they could for firewood. For months, Ehmet's father and the neighbors had been taking pieces of the wood framing from the attic of their apartment building, until they thought that the building might become too weak. Then his father had brought branches he found on his walk home from work at the newspaper. Ehmet and his parents huddled around the leaky woodstove they had rigged up in their kitchen using an old, metal barrel. Smoke blew into the apartment from the damp, green, smoldering branches. When wood was not available, people burned paper—Ehmet's father had burned copies of old articles he had written, "old news"—even shoes and clothes. It was better than being cold.

Ehmet and Milan snuck out of the apartment. As they arrived at the park, they saw people struggling to break off limbs, frantically bending, hacking, sawing, at the fallen trunk. It was their tree. The one they always climbed. The Giant. They stood still and silent as it was carried away. Milan kicked at the sawdust and woodchips left from the sawing and chopping. Ehmet picked up a handful of the tree's wet remains. The chipped wood smelled sweet, with a slight odor of cinnamon, reminding him of his favorite cake his mother used to make, before the war. Ehmet was still thinking about the smell of cake when he heard his father's angry voice.

"What are you doing here?"

"The tree," Ehmet said.

"They cut the last tree," added Milan.

"You know you're not supposed to be here. I was worried about you. Today there were rockets by the newspaper building. Could have been here!"

Ehmet was relieved to find that his father's anger came from concern. Still, he hoped to explain it away. "I know," said Ehmet, "but there was no sniper fire, no rockets here today, and there haven't been on this block for weeks . . . " his voice trailed off. He knew that he was not supposed to be in the park. Yet he had been staying inside their apartment building for most of the last two months, and rockets and rifle fire had struck the building, too. The apartment three doors down from Ehmet's family's had a huge, ragged hole where the front window had been, and large chunks of the walls in what had been the living room were gouged out from an explosion.

Ehmet and Milan had convinced themselves they might be just as safe in the park. But that was not the way Ehmet's father saw it.

"Three people've been killed in this park," said his father. "I want you to be safe, if that is possible. Let's get home." He gripped Ehmet's arm as they walked.

For the first few moments the three of them walked in silence. Then Ehmet started to tell his father about how he and Milan used to climb that tree and what they had seen there, though he didn't tell him how they called out to trick people sometimes. His father's taut face began to soften. Ehmet thought he might understand his feelings about the park. They used to walk there together often.

That night, Ehmet's parents discussed whether or not it would be safer at Aunt Boda and Uncle Petar's farmhouse in the countryside. They had had these discussions before.

"It has been quieter in that part of the country," said his father.

"And Petar is from a Croat family, like mine. Maybe they won't be bothered. Croats haven't been targeted there," noted his mother.

"Targeted. What sense is it anyone being targeted?" said his father.

"Makes no sense to me either, Mirso," said his mother. "Croat, Muslim, Jew, Serb. Suddenly we're so different from each other? Before we were all just Bosnians, together."

"Very together," his father laughed. "Me mostly Muslim—married to you, a Croat."

"And isn't that the way it will stay?" said his mother teasingly.

"As far as I'm concerned, no borders here."

They continued the discussion, unable to decide.

Then a bullet crashed through their living room window and changed the discussion completely.

Ehmet's father ran his hand over the small white crater that the bullet had made in the wall. In the center of the crater a gray lump rested. He touched it and drew his hand back quickly. He blinked his eyes as if awakening from a deep sleep.

"I heard it," said Ehmet's mother. "I heard the bullet whizzing by."

Ehmet had heard it, too. A high-pitched whistle, or what he imagined to be the whining shriek of a banshee.

His father nodded as if going to sleep. Ehmet guessed he was probably thinking of how close the bullet had come for them to have heard it like that, whizzing by their ears. Though it had taken only an instant for the bullet to pass, it filled the space of the entire evening. The bullet had seared their path, and like the moon that could block out the much larger sun, it eclipsed all else.

"The country," said his mother. "Tomorrow morning."

And again, Ehmet saw his father nod.

TWO

◇

The Country

Later that night Ehmet had heard the sounds of his parents' voices in their bedroom, but he could not hear what they were saying. He had fallen asleep, and in the morning was certain he had dreamed of bullets whining like wailing banshees.

Ehmet found his mother struggling to carry her suitcase and a cloth traveling bag into the living room. He wondered what she had packed that was so heavy. He had watched her gather things after the bullet struck the night before. She had looked at framed photographs of the family on the dresser and the walls and had placed a few of those in her suitcase. She had caressed a small vase that her grandmother had given her, put it in carefully among her clothes, and packed the jewelry box that had been a gift from Ehmet's father last year. This wasn't like a vacation trip, where she expected to come home to what she had left. She was taking pieces of home with her.

For Ehmet, packing had not been so complicated. He took his jeans, T-shirt, and running shoes, good for things he liked to do in the countryside—climbing trees or exploring the woods and fields.

For soccer games, if there were any, he packed shorts. Then as an afterthought, he added the better clothes he usually saved for school, in case they stayed for a while. A couple of extra shirts, some underwear, socks, a sweatshirt, a cap—most of what he had not already traded on the streets for food—and that was it for clothes. He decided to pack a notebook and pen, a flashlight, and the pocketknife that his grandfather had given him for his recent birthday—that would be handy in the countryside—and felt he had what he needed. He put in the book that Milan had lent him. Ehmet had promised he would read it. The book was titled *Invasion of the Alien Cashews*, Milan's idea of a funny story. Ehmet wondered when he would see Milan again. Other friends had had to leave suddenly, and he and Milan had talked about that possibility. He hoped Milan would understand.

He had looked around. Maybe he would see none of this again. Remembering what his mother had packed, he leafed through a photo album, took out an old picture of his grandparents in front of their farmhouse in Croatia, and another of his family in the park taken a couple of years ago, and placed the photos between pages of the book to keep them protected. He stuffed the book into his school backpack.

Then he had slept, but had awakened exhausted. He jumped through hoops of thought and got nowhere. He could not picture what was to be, and it was difficult to picture what had been before the chaos of this world-flipped-upside-down. Confusion, he decided, was exhausting.

Ehmet had often gotten through these months by focusing not on trying to make sense of all the world, but only on what was immediately around him. He understood what a fish in dark water might feel like. Through murky waters he also drifted, looking for a clear surface to rise to.

He surfaced now in the living room, his mother's bags and his backpack ready, his parents by the door. But as his eyes scanned every corner of the room, what was missing confirmed what he had suspected. He saw none of his father's bags.

His parents embraced, his mother's head buried in the shoulder of his father's shirt, his father's eyes catching sight of Ehmet.

His father stretched an arm around Ehmet. "I can't go with you two right now, much as I want to. I have to stay . . . the newspaper . . . I'll catch up with you as soon as I can."

Ehmet said nothing. In some ways he understood. They had talked about the newspaper a lot. It was one of the only ways people could find out what was happening each day in Sarajevo. Though there was not always enough paper to print on, the few printed pages were read over and over, passed hand to hand around the city. Even at the rare times the electricity worked, television and radio were increasingly unavailable. Broadcast stations had been blown up or taken over, and there was mainly non-news from the state-run television station—a cooking show when there was no food, or hours of symphony playing the same concerts over and over.

"People have to know," said his father, and tried to explain. If people only knew what was going on, if people understood, things might change.

Ehmet understood that his father was staying here, and he and his mother were going to the country.

First, they would have to thread their way through the city. Now they dodged through backstreets and alleyways with Ehmet's father helping to carry his mother's bags. Gunshots periodically spattered the air at varying distances.

Near their apartment building, the routes were familiar to Ehmet and he helped lead the way. As they made their way farther and farther, the neighborhoods became unfamiliar. His father quickly steered them around this corner, down that wall. He knew these routes well. Ehmet realized then that his father's newspaper work had taken him around the city more than Ehmet had known. He hadn't just been sitting in what little was left of his office building. Perhaps he hadn't said so much to help keep Ehmet or his mother from worrying.

Where they had to cross one intersection, they glimpsed a group of uniformed soldiers down the street. "You three, stop!" one yelled.

"Come on!" Ehmet's father waved his family to a hole in the shattered wall of the nearest building. Ehmet was fastest, out in front. He waited for his mother and father to catch up. "Go!" his father admonished. Ehmet climbed through. The shell that had broken the wall had also destroyed the floor just inside the building. He had no choice but to drop down into the dark basement below. He jumped, unable to judge how far he would fall. Jumping games he had played gave him the experience to know to bend his legs and let them absorb the shock. The floor of the basement caught him quicker than he expected, and he landed stiffer than he liked.

"Down there?" his father called.

"Yeah!"

"Watch it!" His mother's two bags thudded into the basement, followed by his mother who clung to the edge of the wall and lowered herself to drop just a few feet. Ehmet's father jumped to join them. They grabbed the bags, headed toward daylight at the far side of the dim space, and ran up a stairway into an alley. They could hear voices echoing in the basement as they darted along the garbage-strewn alleyway. Dodging around a couple of corners, Ehmet could not help turning to see if the soldiers were following. They seemed to have lost them.

The long walk and run while lugging bags was tiring, rest more and more welcome. From time to time they stopped to catch a breath and shift their bags. Leaning against his backpack, Ehmet sat with his family behind a wall in the remains of yet another abandoned building. Ehmet closed his eyes for a few seconds. Maybe it would all go away. He heard the familiar whistle of a flying shell and snapped alert. He and his friends had learned to tell by the specific sound what kind of shell was incoming, and how close. Some people bet on those things. This one was . . . *KABLOM!*

Bits of concrete, wood, and brick pelted the three. When the hard rain settled, Ehmet opened the eyes he had closed instinctively. Gritty particles scraped and blurred his vision. Becoming conscious of the rest of his body again, he wiggled his arms and legs. As far as he could tell everything was still there. He felt another hand touching one of his arms. He looked hesitantly, not sure what he would see. His mother had reached out to him and was pulling herself up to a sitting position. On the far side of her, his father was brushing off debris. A sliver of wood was speared into one dusty cheek, a red trail running from where it had become embedded.

"Mirso," said Ehmet's mother.

"Everyone okay?" asked his father.

Coughing the dust of the former walls, they examined themselves and each other. Ehmet's father pulled the wood sliver loose from his cheek. The wound it had caused was not large, and appeared to be the worst of the scratches and bruises on the three of them.

They collected themselves and hurried away, driven by the explosion to new haste. Not stopping until they neared the airport, they tucked themselves behind a huge pile of jagged rubble.

Ehmet's father said, "Wait here," and disappeared around a corner.

In a few minutes he returned with a man in street clothes who had an automatic rifle cradled in front of him. "This is them?"

"Yes," said Ehmet's father. "He'll take you." He indicated the armed man to Ehmet and his mother.

The four of them approached the gaping, dark mouth of a tunnel. An assortment of armed men, some in uniforms, others in scruffy outfits like they might have worn to work on a construction site, milled around the opening. The tunnel used to carry water. Now humans trickled through. Some people called it "The Tunnel of Life." With no buses or planes, the only escape route went through the earth rather than above it.

A few of the men by the tunnel entrance eyed the four. Ehmet and his mother's armed guide nodded, and waved them off. Some acted as if they did not see Ehmet's family.

Ehmet's father hugged Ehmet and his mother. "I'll miss you," his father said.

"C'mon, we have to go," their armed guide grumbled at Ehmet and his mother. Surrounded by an edgy group of armed men, Ehmet had to admit this was not the most appealing place to linger.

His father took a few steps with them into the dark tunnel. "Just the two from here on," the guide said to him.

"I'll see you. Soon," Ehmet's father said, and stopped walking. When Ehmet turned to look back, he could make out his father's silhouette in the light of the tunnel entrance, waving.

"Stay close," said the armed man, flipping on a flashlight to spear the dark.

Ehmet and his mother picked their way along with him, feet splashing in occasional puddles on the tunnel floor, the rounded walls of the tunnel more sensed than seen in the darkness. A couple of times flashlights bobbed toward them, reminding Ehmet of walks in the night on camping trips he'd taken. These lights, though, were ominous. Ehmet worried who might be approaching. The guide only muttered to him "Keep moving."

Shadowy figures, humpbacked with backpacks and satchels, hurried by without speaking, heading toward the Sarajevo Ehmet and his mother had fled.

A glimmer in the distance became a full, round, plate of light as the three of them neared the end of the tunnel. The guide hustled them outside to a town bustling with armed and unarmed traders, dealing treasures Ehmet had not partaken of in many months— piles of tinned and fresh food heaped on the ground or in the open backs of small trucks and cars, or being loaded into packs for the journey through the tunnel. These black marketers were hustling goods toward Sarajevo as refugees struggled to leave.

Their guide prodded Ehmet and his mother on, giving them no time to stop and purchase any of the treasured goods. He wove through the streets trying to find someone he knew who had a car and would be willing to take them farther into the countryside. Cars were scarce, gasoline scarcer. Like almost everything else, gasoline was hard to come by and cost many times what it had before. The same men who were doing the shooting controlled the buying and selling and movement of what was for sale—gasoline, food, clothes. People said that was one of the main reasons the shooting kept on like it did, because it was profitable.

Very few people still drove cars, and it was difficult to find some-one willing to use precious gas and face the dangers of the road as well. But for enough German marks or American dollars, things could be bought.

After their guide found them a ride, he left, saying only "Good luck."

With Ehmet, his mother, and the luggage stuffed into the tiny car, legs and arms tucked here and there, there was little room to move. The driver guessed, or perhaps knew, which back roads were the best bets to take. No one talked. Silence on this journey seemed safer. Ehmet was damp with nervous sweat cooling on his body, and he could smell the apprehension of the driver in front of him. Each curve rounded without trouble brought easier breaths.

Fortunately, it was not such a long ride to Ehmet's aunt and uncle's house, and when they arrived Ehmet was relieved to be in the quiet countryside without the sounds of shells, rockets, and bullets that chipped at each day in Sarajevo. On the other hand, he wanted to run back to the city where friends and his father remained. He felt as if he had deserted them, as if he should have stayed in the city no matter what. But his feet stayed planted on the country earth. He took a deep breath, the first breath he was conscious of taking since leaving the city, and to his surprise, found that although so much had changed, the air still smelled like country air.

In the yard, Ehmet saw apples covering a tree, looking like a rich oasis of food after the many months of scarcity in the city. Luci the cat cruised her world as she always had and rubbed Ehmet's leg as if they were old friends. Aunt Boda and Uncle Petar ran to greet them. The driver pulled away as soon as Ehmet and his mother had their things out of the car.

After they brought their bags in, were fed fresh bread, cheese, sweet farm preserves, and had caught up somewhat in a torrent of conversation, Ehmet left the adults chatting and sipping tea, and wandered back into the yard. He scratched Luci behind the ears and admired the apple tree. When he plucked what appeared to be one of the ripest apples from a branch and sunk his teeth into it, bittersweet drops of juice exploded in his mouth. The fruit was not quite ripe yet. He devoured the apple anyway, only stopping to avoid the brown spot where a caterpillar curled, nestled at home in the core. When he was younger, Ehmet would have quit eating after the first fairly bitter bite. But he was thirteen now and could stand a bit of bitter mixed with the sweet.

THREE

◇

Game

Ehmet couldn't wait to explore, to look for his friends from his visits here before.

"Be careful," his mother said as he left. Yet she let him go without the extended discussion they would have had in the city. For the first time in many months his mother seemed to feel safer, too.

It felt good to walk. At first Ehmet found himself scurrying hurriedly between trees, ducking behind them then pausing to look around, until he accustomed himself to hearing no gunfire—to believing that there were no snipers here.

He inhaled richly again, smelled damp, fall earth, and the musty smells of leaves, decaying remnants of summer's growing season. He walked by fields that would usually have been full of vegetables ready to harvest or rows just harvested with their remaining shriveled pieces of plants scattered across the long furrows. On the farm he was nearing, Sami, one of the boys Ehmet played soccer with whenever he visited his aunt and uncle, would be helping with the harvest at this time of year, digging potatoes from a field or guiding the wheel of the tractor as his father threw hay onto the wagon behind it. Last fall they had let Ehmet drive the tractor for the first time and laughed as the machine wobbled across the field.

"Keep it in the field. No racing for the highway," Sami's father had chuckled while he and Sami heaped hay onto the wagon.

"You headed for the coast?" Sami had teased, as Ehmet turned wide around the corner of the field and headed west, in the direction of the distant Adriatic Sea. "You're tired of this mountain life and heading for the beach?"

"You have your bathing suit on, right?" Ehmet had called over the thunking roar of the tractor engine.

"With you driving, I have to be ready for anything," Sami had rung back.

This year, the same fields were filled with weeds. Instead of neat rows, ragged tufts of plants going to seed and a few silvery wildflowers made a shaggy carpet. As Ehmet approached the open doors of the shed where the tractor was kept, he looked anxiously inside.

A few old tools were strewn on the floor where the tractor should have been. As Ehmet turned to leave the shed, an eerie shadow caught his eye. It was the pitchfork usually used for hay, in a position he had never seen a pitchfork. It was stuck in the back wall like a spear might stick in a tree. The long handle was suspended parallel to the floor, the sharp tines embedded deep in the wooden wall. Ehmet had handled this pitchfork and knew that it would have had to be thrown with great force to stick in the wall like that. He felt a chill. He could not imagine Sami or his father throwing the pitchfork; he had never seen them use it as anything but a tool. Ehmet wondered who had thrown it.

He turned, walked to the house, and knocked on the front door. No one answered. While he waited and strained to hear footsteps or noise within, he noticed below the doorknob a large nail angled through the wooden door and into the frame around it. He looked up, and saw a similar spike near the top of the door. The door had been nailed shut. No one could go in or out without removing the spikes or breaking through the door. Ehmet went back down the two doorsteps, walked over to what he knew was one of the living room windows, and stretched himself to peer inside.

Only filtered sunlight from the windows lit the room. Ehmet could see the sofa, a couple of chairs, the furniture in the room more or less as he remembered it. But the space looked barren. The small things that Ehmet had been used to seeing, plates on the tabletops, pictures on the walls, shoes or Sami's soccer ball on the floor by the door were missing. The room had been stripped. It was a shell that no longer contained those who had made it home before, like the snail shells that Ehmet picked up in gardens—translucent, uninhabited, with a fragile brittleness that might shatter at the next touch.

Bright shafts of light from the windows fell across the room. Ehmet saw that the floor was covered with dust, as it had never been when Sami's family was there. They had kept the tile floors shining, and padded through the glistening house in slippers or socks. No footprints marked the dust. Sami's family had not walked here for some time.

Ehmet did not walk. He ran from the house. It felt haunted, spooky. He turned his head to look back every couple of steps as he ran. No ghosts appeared to be chasing him. When he rounded a hill and a turn in the road and the house disappeared from view, he stopped running. He was breathing heavily from the exertion. He felt weak. He had been one of the fastest long-distance runners in his class at school, yet today he wondered if he could even keep up with those who had been last in the races. "Probably from not eating so much," he thought. Everyone else in his class was likely in the same predicament, though it was hard to imagine a hungry Darko. "Fee, fi, fo, fum," he pictured bulky Darko, a scowling giant from some fable banging silverware on a table, calling for food.

When Ehmet arrived at his friend Ivan's farm, Ivan's father was out in a field with a horse-drawn wagon, pulling a heaped-up load of straw for the animals to the barn.

"Hello, Ehmet!" Ivan's father called. "What are you doing here? It's not summer vacation you know . . . " he added with a laugh. Ivan's father sometimes had what Ehmet and Ivan called a strange sense of humor. But Ehmet was glad that he at least still had a sense of humor.

"I know, I know."

"Well, you're welcome here," said Ivan's father.

Ehmet always had felt welcome at Ivan's, as he had with almost all of the other families in this part of Bosnia when he had visited. It was a small community, and everyone knew each other. Most were friends. Ehmet knew that Ivan's father and Sami's father had grown up together and were close.

"What happened to Sami's family?" he asked.

"They left," said Ivan's father. "You know, they're Muslims. Some of the wild ones threatened them. Said they weren't welcome here anymore. Weren't welcome? That family didn't need a welcome, they were already here, got roots here hundreds of years old."

"Wild ones?" Ehmet wondered.

"Some of those that call themselves Serbs, in this case. They call me a Croat. Which maybe I am if the package needs a brand, but I'd rather simply call myself a human being, to tell you the truth." He paused. "What's your family doing here?"

"Just me and my mother," said Ehmet.

"The newspaper?"

"Yes."

"Well, we need the newspaper."

"I know." But knowing didn't make the situation better in this case, Ehmet thought.

"We've been wondering how you all were doing in Sarajevo. What we hear is not so good."

"Lots of people have been leaving."

"Here, too. I don't know whether we're the fools to stay, or the fools to leave."

Ehmet wasn't sure himself. He didn't say anything.

"Ivan's in the house. I'm sure he'll be glad to see you."

Ivan was pleased to see Ehmet. They spoke as if they had seen each other just yesterday, even if there were many new twists to before and after. That was one of the good things about Ivan. Ehmet and he could go months without seeing each other and continue on as if there had been no break.

Ivan's mother gave them each a piece of cake and a glass of milk from one of the farm's cows. Ehmet was starting to feel more certain that it would be different here.

"Careful," added Ivan's mother as Ivan and Ehmet took off to try to gather enough people for a soccer game. But she let them go, too. No warnings about which routes to take, or today's shelling. War seemed distant.

On the path, Ehmet and Ivan jogged along, kicking and passing the soccer ball between them. When they reached the end of Ivan's farm's fields, Ehmet turned left. Ivan stopped and gave Ehmet a puzzled look.

"Where are you going?" Ivan asked.

"To Zoran's," said Ehmet. "Isn't he around?"

"Yes, but . . . "

"So?"

"His family's Serb," said Ivan.

"Serbs don't play soccer?"

"Not with us."

"Oh, come on," said Ehmet. Zoran had been friends with them for as long as Ehmet could remember. "Let's see," Ehmet waved him on.

"I don't think he'll be able to play," said Ivan.

When they got to Zoran's, Ivan stopped by the wall that enclosed the yard.

"I'm not going up there."

"You've been here a thousand times. What's the big deal?"

"His parents . . . no, I'm not going."

"So wait then," said Ehmet.

He saw movement inside the house as he approached the door. He knocked. Nothing happened. He knocked again, several times. The door opened, but only a crack. Ehmet could see the shadow of Zoran's mother standing there.

"What do you want?" she said finally.

"It's me, Ehmet."

"I see that."

Ehmet was taken aback at the harshness of her voice, but he continued. "We just wanted to see if Zoran wants to play soccer."

"Not today. He has things to do." She closed the door.

Ehmet walked back to Ivan.

"That's the way it is now," said Ivan. He started to walk away.

Ehmet turned to look back at the house, and saw Zoran in an upstairs window.

"Look," Ehmet said. But by the time Ivan had turned to look, Zoran had disappeared.

Eventually they found enough of their old friends to have a game. At a few houses they got responses similar to the closed door at Zoran's, but at others they were welcomed, or at least not chased away. Though most of the players were from families that might call themselves Croat, some were from Serb or Muslim families—there were players of all kinds, including Jaca, who played soccer as well as any of the boys. She dribbled the ball around players as if they were standing still, which a few were, but she had the running speed and quick moves to play soccer with the best of the boys. "Goal!" she shouted as she shot past Ivan.

Seeing her play, Ehmet thought of Mira, who had been one of the best soccer players in his class. Last spring she had come back to school after having been absent for several months. She came hopping on crutches, with one of her legs missing. "A shell," she said simply, and most of the class tried to act as if they did not notice, that nothing had changed, hoping that by not noticing perhaps somehow it would not be so. Some could not help crying, and tried to turn from her to hide tears. Then they all sat, unusually quiet, wondering if they might be next. That afternoon, as Mira made her way up the aisle toward the blackboard at the front of the room, Darko silently lifted his chair closer to the aisle. He thrust his foot into the aisle—just in time to catch the tip of one of Mira's crutches. "Muslim pig," it sounded like Darko had muttered as she stumbled. She pitched forward toward the floor, but before anyone could react to what was happening, she planted one crutch out in front of herself to stop her descent and swung the other around in a great arc that struck Darko's chest with such force that the whole class could hear its impact. His chair squeaked backward.

Darko sat stunned, as did the rest of the class. Their teacher, Mrs. Barisic, hearing the sounds, had turned to face them from the blackboard, where she had been writing the problem Mira was on her way to answer.

"What happened?" Mrs. Barisic asked.

No one spoke. Studying the silent, stunned faces of the class she said, "All right, we'll take this up later."

Mira had continued on her way to the front of the room. She solved the problem on the board, then stared at Darko.

At recess that day everyone in the class was amazed when Mira, after standing on the sidelines of the soccer game for a while said "I want to play," and hopped onto the field with her crutches and swung her foot at the ball. She missed, and almost fell. When she regained her balance, she swung her foot and this time connected. The ball shot downfield. "I know I can't play like before," she said as she hopped aside to let the teams continue, "but I'm not going to stop living."

Before the fighting had started and Mira got injured, at the first and only school dance, most of the boys and girls had stood talking uneasily. Mira had grabbed Ehmet's hand and said, "Let's go. Let's face the music and dance."

Embarrassed, Ehmet had hesitated. But she did not let go of his hand. She tugged and he accompanied her. She and Ehmet had swung and swayed on the otherwise empty dance floor. After that, the floor had filled with dancers, and the mood changed. For all the brave talk of the boys, Mira was one of the bravest people Ehmet knew.

Today it was Zoran who wanted to show his willingness to face the possible music. Shortly after Ehmet, Ivan, and the rest of the crew had started the game, Zoran showed up at a run, panting.

"Zoran! How did you know where we were going?" Ehmet called.

"The soccer ball you guys were kicking around was a clue," he laughed. Besides, they had always played at this field. "You think I'd miss this game? We hardly play these days."

"How did you get out?" Ivan asked.

"Snuck out."

"What if your parents find out?"

"They won't know where I went. And if they figure it out . . . you guys are not my enemy."

Ivan and Ehmet nodded in agreement, though with worried looks. They weren't concerned for themselves, but both could picture what might happen to Zoran. They had seen his father pull his belt from his pants and hit Zoran with it before. That was just one possibility. Zoran was taking a big risk. Yet that was, he said, his own decision.

The game went on all that afternoon, until players started drifting away for dinner. Ehmet could feel his body giving out a bit. His endurance was not what it had been, yet the thrills of the game and being with his old friends carried him forward. It was a great game, and he walked back to his aunt and uncle's house elated.

He told his mother and aunt and uncle about the match. "It's good that some things haven't changed," said his mother. "At least you can still enjoy a game with your friends."

He was pleased about the afternoon and tired, so he went to bed early and slept soundly.

Ehmet awoke with a start. He heard three loud thuds—*thunk, thunk, thunk*—and pictured a green-uniformed arm with a hard fist pounding on the door of the house. Someone was out there trying to get in.

He lifted himself from the pillow and carefully eased up a corner of the old curtain. It was still dark outside, well into the night, with no sign of morning. Through the curtain slit he could see a bit of the clay tile roof that extended over the first floor of the house. Below that was the wrinkled, metal shed roof sloping into the backyard. He raised his head farther and could see most of the backyard with its two trees, splotchy shadows in the light of a bright fingernail of a moon. He saw nothing moving.

Ehmet listened for a voice calling to him. When they first arrived at the farm, he and his mother had agreed on the code words "Water man, water man." If he heard her using those words he would know that this was an emergency. But he did not hear her voice, or any sounds inside the house.

He stared outside again. Apples dangled in clumps on the tree next to the shed. A gust of wind pushed hard at the rustling tree branches. They arched and sprang back sharply as the wind eased. *Thunk, thunk.* More noises shivered the darkness. Ehmet could just make out a dark dot bouncing down the ridges of the shed roof, then over the edge into the backyard. A creature skittered out of the shadows below and into the moonlight. It was the cat, Luci. Like Ehmet, she had been frightened by the sudden loud noises in the night.

"Just apples falling," Ehmet whispered to himself.

He pulled the curtain back a little farther and watched Luci scamper into the shadows under the apple tree and disappear. Ehmet strained his eyes to see anything else moving in the countryside night. There was no movement and no more sound except the swishing of the trees.

He lowered the curtain and lay his head back onto the pillow. He closed his eyes, and noted the anxious stiffness of his body, all his muscles tight. Ehmet tried to relax. His thoughts kept returning to his father and the city miles away, until after much tossing he fell asleep again.

The next sounds he became aware of were frantic shouts from downstairs.

◇

FOUR

Across the Roof

"**W**ater man, water man!" he heard his mother call out.

"What are you doing?" a gruff, unfamiliar voice shouted.

Ehmet slipped out of bed and walked on his toes to the doorway of his room. Downstairs, he could hear the voices of his aunt and uncle, but they were speaking in softer tones and volume so he could not make out what they were saying.

He heard several other strange voices yelling. One said, "Here!" And then there were crashes of glass breaking.

"Hey!" Uncle Petar's voice called.

A jumble of shouting voices from which Ehmet could distinguish little mixed with a terrible rumble of sounds, clattering heavy objects that Ehmet imagined might be furniture being thrown around, wood splintering. Ehmet's first impulse was to run downstairs to see what was happening and help if he could.

But when he heard his mother again call "Water man!" this time more desperately, he was prodded toward what he was supposed to do. "Remember," his mother had said, "if ever you hear me calling 'Water man,' run! Whatever you think is happening, go. I'll meet you, like we've agreed."

Ehmet grabbed his pants from the back of the chair and pulled them on. He stuck his feet into the running shoes that lay on the floor next to his backpack, which he also threw on.

He had kneeled to quickly tie a flapping shoelace when he heard footsteps pounding up the stairs, accompanied by unfamiliar shouting voices. He looked toward the door. The only way out now was the window. He sprang to it and pushed the window open. The backpack caught on the window frame, and as he tugged it free he tumbled onto the roof outside. His own breathing sounded to Ehmet like throttling winds and his heartbeat like booming drumbeats in the night air, yet in the house he could hear the footsteps and shouts in the hall coming closer. He thought for a moment about continuing to lie there under the window, but anyone looking out could see him. He leaped up and dashed across the roof, away from the window, hoping that no one would spot him and that the sounds of his running would be covered by the storm of noises coming from inside the house. As he pulled himself over a peak of the roof and out of view of the window, he heard shouts and thuds in the room he had just left.

He paused for a moment to listen. At any instant he expected someone would realize where he was. Yet from what he could hear, no one seemed to have spotted him. In a crouch he continued down the roof, trying to grip the damp, slick, pitched surface with the flat soles of his shoes. He could feel himself slipping, and lowered his backside to the roof. The cloth of his pants gave him more traction. His slide stopped, and he caught himself at the roof edge. He peered over. Convincing himself that he had jumped from this height on other occasions, he leaped. There was no time to think about the fall. Before he could consider it further, he had thumped to earth.

"Someone is out there!" he heard a slurred, drunken sounding voice call from upstairs.

He scrambled along the wall out of view of the house, to the far end of the shed. Luci was there. She was frightened by the hulk running toward her, and took off across the yard.

Blam, blam. Two shots boomed. Ehmet felt as if the reverberations moved the air around him.

But the shots had been fired when Luci ran into view of the house. "It's a damn cat!" he heard someone yell.

Ehmet's instinct was to get as far from the shooting as he could. Opposite the yard that Luci had crossed was a field. He guessed that the shed partially blocked the view from the house to the field. Keeping the shed between himself and the house, hoping again that he would not be seen, he bent to make himself less visible, and ran.

The backpack bounced on his spine. Ehmet felt like a turtle carrying his humped shell with him, and as slow as one. It seemed to take forever to cross the open field though it was only seconds. He was glad to have the backpack on. It felt like protection, as if it would shield him from bullets. He knew it wouldn't, yet it was reassuring to have something between him and the house.

He did not stop running until he reached the far edge of the field.

◇

FIVE

Meeting Place

Every instant, he waited for the clatter of gunshots. But there were none.

He dropped to the ground, rolled over, and after catching his breath, parted the high grass so that he could look back at the house. It was good he had decided to run in this direction. The shed blocked much of the direct view to and from the house, though he could see bands of light from a couple of the windows. Inside, a man moved quickly by a window in the living room. He was in uniform. It was not Uncle Petar.

Even at this distance, he could hear shouting in the house. He strained to make out whose voices the shouts belonged to, and to hear the words they were saying. The walls of the house muffled the voices. What he could hear was a series of sounds that were indistinct except in their unusual harshness of tones: thumping, screeching, and wailing in extended, staccato bursts. A couple of doors slammed. Ehmet considered going back to the house.

He listened, yet did not want to hear. His thoughts bounced from image to image, trying to picture what might be going on in the house. The more terrible images he tried to chase away as quickly as they appeared.

Suddenly he realized that he was hearing no sounds. At first he thought it was because he had not been listening, not been hearing, because of all the noise in his head. He quieted himself, focused again, and found that the night was silent. He lay still and listening for a time. He did not know whether hours or minutes had passed.

When he was certain it had been quite some time since he had heard anything, he thought of the agreement with his mother and of their meeting place. Perhaps she was already there. Ehmet leaped up and started running to the appointed spot.

Ehmet ran as if the night itself might close around and lock him in. He tried to outrun it, to burst out of it. Being outside at night in the countryside was familiar from the camping trips he had taken almost every summer. This was not familiar. This night brought no friendly comfort, only hopes of getting beyond the reach of what had happened and whoever might be chasing him.

He did not look back until he reached the huge, white-barked plane tree by the river, where he and his mother had agreed to meet. No one was visible behind him. He peered around the tree, looking for his mother. She was not there. Tentatively he peeked into the hollow at the base of the tree, hoping somehow to find her sitting there.

They had sat under this tree many times, mostly in the warmer weather. When he was little, Ehmet had hidden in the tree hollow and laughed in delight when his mother "found" him there. In recent years, Ehmet often came to the river to fish. On the occasions that his mother had been here, too, she had sat, relaxed, against the tree, watching the river drift by.

Tonight she was nowhere to be seen. Ehmet thought about going to search for her, but for the moment decided to wait here as they'd agreed. She had insisted. "Wait for me there. Don't move. Then I'll know where to find you."

He sat and leaned against the tree. The chill of the fall night air soon penetrated the clothes he had thrown on when he escaped the house. Ehmet touched the pack still on his back, cushioning him against the tree. He was glad he'd grabbed it and that it still contained much of what he had brought to the countryside. He reached into the pack, dug out his sweatshirt, and pulled it over his head as quickly as he could so as not to miss seeing or hearing anything.

For a while he just waited. From time to time he heard what he thought might be footsteps. Once a twig cracked. He stiffened his body attentively, searched the night in anticipation, but neither his mother nor anyone else appeared. He looked at the sky and found a few of the constellations he knew, Leo, Little Bear, and the North Star: Ehmet would know where north was. At least something was there as it had been before. The stars moved, though in a much different time. He remembered what his teacher, Mrs. Barisic, had said. Because stars are at such tremendous distances from Earth, when we see them what we are seeing is starlight from millions of years ago, the light takes that long to reach us.

The events of the night had tired him, but he did not want to sleep. He wrapped his arms around his knees and dropped his head to rest. Even with the sweatshirt on, the cold seeped in. He pulled his body into a ball, but there was no way to keep warm.

Ehmet thought of all the times he had curled up in the hollow of the tree. He crawled in there. It was snug, and whether from his memories or from the heat of his body held in the small cave, he felt a bit warmer. He listened for his mother, and occasionally stuck his head out to see what he could. As the sky lightened he had an unexpected visitor.

A patch of fur brushed one of his hands. Shocked, his body jolted upright and he bumped his head against the roof of the tree hollow. There was no room to move inside the tree trunk. He started to scramble out, and found himself face-to-face with someone he knew: the cat.

"Luci!" The first word he had said aloud that night. She had followed or found him. It didn't matter which. He cradled her in his arms and scratched behind her ears. He did not feel so alone now.

Ehmet kept himself awake, periodically shifting his body around to try to keep comfortable in the small space. After a while Luci leaped out of his arms, and he looked outside to see if she had stayed nearby. He couldn't see her. From the changing color of the sky he knew dawn was approaching. He thought about going back to the farmhouse. That seemed an even worse idea now that it was becoming light. It would be difficult to stay out of sight of any armed men who might still be around.

Then he heard footsteps. It sounded like one person, walking noisily. He cautiously eased his head out of the tree hollow just enough to peer toward the sounds.

His mother stumbled toward the tree.

"Mom!" he said as he scrambled out and ran toward her.

She hugged him. But she did not say anything. She just sobbed.

SIX

Away

"**What** happened?" Ehmet asked.

His mother pulled away. Her eyes, glazed and dull, showed none of their usual sparkle. Ehmet could smell sour sweat and alcohol, smells which he did not recognize as hers. He noticed scratches on her face and a bruise around one eye. There was a patch of dried blood by her nose. She turned and stared at the river.

Before Ehmet could figure out what was happening, she had taken the few steps to reach the river's edge. He thought she would stop there, but she kept walking. She walked right into the water until it swirled around her waist. Her long skirt floated up to the surface in a circle surrounding her.

"Mom!" he called again.

She reached for the river, threw water up onto her face and kept splashing it onto her arms and jacket, rubbing as if she were trying to scrub clean.

Ehmet was now at the river's edge wading in, the water just up over the rubber soles of his shoes.

"Mom!"

She turned, waded back toward him, and collapsed on the riverbank.

Ehmet crouched next to her and put his arm across her shoulders and his face close to hers.

"Mom, what's wrong?" She stayed silent, locked inside herself. Ehmet could see in the early daylight that her skin was pale, and blue around her lips. She was cold, and her wet clothes chilled her further. She shivered, and Ehmet felt a chill not from the cold night but from seeing her like this.

Ehmet's thoughts were interrupted by the rumbling of a vehicle coming up the road from the direction of the farmhouse. It was still distant. To Ehmet it sounded like the throaty bellow of a truck.

There were enough trees and brush between where he and his mother huddled on the riverbank and the road so that they would not likely be seen by anyone passing. He looked up at the nearby bridge, over which the road crossed the river. They could be seen easily from the bridge.

"Mom! Mom!" She did not respond. He shook her shoulder gently.

"Mom, we have to move. They might see us." He had said they, not someone. It was the men from last night he was thinking about. It seemed she might be thinking the same. She pushed herself to her feet with Ehmet's help. She hesitated. The truck rumbled closer.

They bolted the few yards up the riverbank to the bridge, his mother stumbling along the way. Ehmet pulled her with him into the shadows under the bridge just as the truck rattled above their heads. Singing voices rang out in choppy bits over the truck's noise. Ehmet had heard the song before, a Serb anthem about the greatness of the Serb people. His mother shuddered and collapsed again.

Ehmet listened as the truck continued on and its sounds faded to nothing. The only noises were the quiet lapping of the river against rocks and his mother's heavy breathing. "Mom, what do you want to do?"

"Go," she said softly.

"Where?"

"Away," she said, much more firmly.

"What about Aunt Boda and Uncle Petar?"

"Taken. Put on a truck. I ran." She turned from Ehmet and covered her face with her arm.

He waited, but his mother stayed crumpled and silent.

Ehmet made as sure as he could that no one else was around and ran back to the tree to get the backpack he had left in the hollow. When he reached in to grab the pack, Luci appeared and pattered into the hollowed tree trunk.

"We're not staying, Luci," said Ehmet, reaching to pet her.

She followed him back under the bridge. His mother did not appear to have moved.

"Mom, where are we going to go?"

She did not answer. She sat on the muddy bank, hunched against the rock-wall foundations of the bridge. On a stone next to her he spotted a knotted tangle of discarded fishing line. He inspected it. No hook. The months of wartime in the city had sharpened his alertness both to danger and to what might be useful. He stuffed the tangle into a pocket.

It was cold in the shadows. Neither his mother nor Ehmet would be comfortable here. Ehmet would have to figure out what to do next.

The first thing was to get his mother warmed up, and hopefully she would start talking more. Ehmet thought about the nearby possibilities. Going back to Aunt Boda and Uncle Petar's house didn't seem like a good idea—Ehmet didn't know what or who he might find there. Until his mother said more all he knew was that she wanted to go away. No one who Ehmet knew lived close to the bridge. It was far from certain that he and his mother would be welcomed by strangers. So that was out. The friends he had played soccer with would be a good bet. But they all lived back in the direction of Aunt Boda and Uncle Petar's farm.

Another truck or perhaps the same one as before, with raucous shouters, rattled over the bridge in the direction that led to his friends' houses. That made staying on their own seem the best idea at the moment.

Ehmet looked out from under the bridge. A few hundred yards

farther up the river he could see the top of an old barn. He had
seen the barn many times before, and its familiarity was comforting. It sat by the ruins of an abandoned farmhouse, surrounded
by fields, quite a distance from the nearest inhabited houses. At
least it might be a place to dry out and warm up.

"Come on, Mom." Ehmet put his arm around her back, and
she rose slowly to her feet. He led her along the river edge. The
river had worn away the land, so the top of the bank next to them
was higher than their heads. They could not easily be seen from
the surrounding land or the road unless someone was crossing
the bridge. Ehmet listened for traffic and kept turning around to
make sure no one was watching them from the bridge.

Following the river, they made their way toward the barn,
rounding bends along the shore. They stepped over a litter of
empty, plastic bottles. In a narrow place in the river, a sea of bottle bottoms in blues, greens, and clear bobbed between the banks.
For some strange reason, people had taken the trouble to secure
the caps onto most of the bottles before trashing them. Since the
war had started, garbage—particularly plastic bottles—had been
thrown with abandon as if it no longer mattered where they fell.
Here it seemed to Ehmet as if not only Bosnia had thrown its bottles, the rest of Europe had added theirs as well.

Ehmet was desperately thirsty. He knew, though, that the river
water, clear as it appeared, was likely a rich soup of bacteria and
other added surprises. He picked up a clean-looking empty bottle from the litter. Later it might hold a better drink.

The barn was a good choice. There was plenty of old hay, and
his mother immediately lay in a pile of it. He pushed more hay
around her. The hay was browned, had been here for some time,
and there were no tools or evidence of recent activity. It did not
look like anyone had been using the barn lately. Ehmet crossed
back to the barn door and checked outside. He had a clear view
across the fields and would be able to see anyone approaching.

He returned and sat next to his mother. She took his hand and
smiled weakly, her first smile since she had found him at the tree.
Her clothes were still damp and cool. She had brought nothing
with her except the wet clothes she was wearing.

Ehmet took off his backpack, opened it, and looked inside. Among his clothes were a few things that might fit her. He took out his fleece pullover and a T-shirt. They would do for her upper body, but her skirt was the wettest from her walk into the river. He dug around for the pair of good pants he'd packed when they had first left home. He held them up. They should fit. He and his mother had been almost the same size for the past few months as Ehmet had grown taller and she had gotten smaller, skinnier anyway, since they hadn't been eating well.

His mother reached over and touched the clothes.

"Here, Mom, put them on."

"You'll need them," she said.

"You need them. At least 'til yours are dry. What I've got on is warm and dry. I'm fine."

Ehmet walked over to the barn door to check outside while she changed. He saw no one out there, and the countryside seemed disturbingly silent, as if everyone had abandoned it, or was in hiding like his mother and him.

"What do you think?" he heard her say. He turned toward her.

"You feel warmer?"

"Yes." She sounded a little more relaxed. She had changed clothes and was curled in the hay again, her wet clothes piled next to her.

Ehmet used a damp edge of her skirt to gently wipe stains and bits of dried blood from the bruises on her face. She winced. He drew back.

"It's okay," she said, and closed her eyes. Within moments she had fallen into an exhausted sleep.

Ehmet sat by her, listening to the heavy sounds of her breathing, and thinking. He still didn't know where they would go. His stomach rumbled. He remembered that he had not eaten since yesterday, and his mouth clacked, dry with thirst.

Long ago were the days when he had a candy bar or snack in his backpack. For the past months any food he had was usually eaten right away. And a candy bar was a luxury from another planet, unattainable except in imagination. Ehmet wondered what candy bars would be eaten on Saturn. "The Ringed

Thing"—he imagined a sweet bar wrapped in layers of different flavors. But those reveries did not last long. The noises from his stomach called out for something to be done beyond imagining.

Ehmet thought about what they might eat. They had no food with them. Okay. There were no shops close by, and besides, Ehmet had only a few coins. He thought again about seeking one of his friends for help. That would mean walking quite a distance away and possible encounters with the men in the trucks. Not knowing who was still wandering in the area or why, he wanted to stay hidden as much as possible, which left finding food close to the barn.

Ehmet was concerned about leaving his mother here. But she was sleeping soundly, and he decided that he would not go out of sight of the barn. Because of the openness of the area around the building, he could keep watch from outside as he looked for food and if he saw anyone headed toward the barn, he would return immediately and was almost certain that he could get there before them.

Before leaving, Ehmet picked up the pile of his mother's wet clothes and carried them up to the loft. He spread them out on the hay in front of the only window. The light streaming in broke the chill of the night and early morning. Ehmet lingered briefly enjoying the warmth, then climbed down from the loft.

He took a pen and his spiral notebook from his backpack, tore a page from the book, and wrote a note to his mother in case she woke up while he was gone. Folding the note, he stuck it in the pocket of the pullover so that most of it was still visible. It fanned out under her chin. She would be sure to find it. He repacked the backpack and hid it under a pile of hay. Carefully piling more hay over his mother, he covered her except for a small opening around her head so that she could breathe. She was so deep in the pile of hay that her head was only visible if Ehmet stood directly above her. It would be difficult for someone to see her unless they already knew she was here.

He went outside to a corner of the barn and peered in all directions. The closest neighboring farmhouse sat at quite a distance, across two fields. He saw no one. The field adjoining the barn was overgrown with waist-high plants. It hadn't been planted this year and didn't seem to offer much possibility for finding food. At the far end of the field, near a stone wall that separated the field from the road, were three gnarly old apple trees with leaves mostly fallen. A few apples still bobbed in the wind on the near-naked branches. After the months of not having eaten fruit, apples still appealed to Ehmet and his stomach. An open barrel next to the barn, full to the brim with rainwater, distracted him momentarily. Using both hands as a cup he dipped and drank his fill, then returned with the bottle he'd found by the river, rinsed and filled it.

Then Ehmet bent over so that the high grasses shielded him from view and made his way through the field toward the apple trees. A thorny berry bush caught one leg of his pants, and the few berries remaining on it caught his eye. He pulled the berries from the bush. They were beyond ripe, and watery from standing in the autumn damp, though still edible. A little farther along, as he pushed his way through the grasses, he saw a potato plant that had managed to establish itself among the wild plants. Ehmet knew, from times he had spent at his grandparents' farm in Croatia, that potato plants would come up in fields where they had been planted as a crop years before. When harvesting potatoes it was impossible to dig every last one from a field, so even one small potato left in the earth could later grow into a plant such as this. His grandparents had taught him a lot about plants, especially when they had seen he was interested in growing things. Now he was glad he knew about digging potatoes. To mark the spot he looked at the surrounding plants, fuzzy-leafed mullein good to make tea for coughs, and shiny plantain that could take the sting from bites. He would dig the potatoes later.

Just before he got to the apple trees he heard the abrupt sound of a vehicle's engine starting. He dropped flat on his stomach. A few plants poked underneath him. He listened, and beyond the crunching of the plants as he wriggled to get more comfortable, he heard the deep thumping of the engine. It was a tractor, probably a couple of farms away. Not a vehicle he needed to be concerned about unless it moved closer.

He scrambled the remaining few feet to the apple trees. Beneath them, he found a bumpy scattering of apples that had fallen from the branches. Many were already browned and mushy, starting to ferment, with a pungent yet not altogether unpleasant and still-fruity smell. Ehmet found some that were firm, and turned them to find any telltale holes where insects might have entered. The apples that appeared best, he placed in a small pile. Soon there were as many as he thought he could carry. He stuffed a couple into his pants pockets, then pulled off his sweatshirt. He tied the sleeves together to close one end of the shirt, making it into a bag.

As he leaned over, focusing all of his attention on getting the apples into the makeshift bag, a car whizzed by on the road. Ehmet was startled. He had missed hearing it coming, its engine noise drowned out by the tractor, and his focus on the apples. It was too late to hide. The car had already passed him, and who-ever was in it would have already seen him.

Ehmet looked over the stone wall at the edge of the field to see the small car racing in the direction of the city. As the car rounded a bend in the road, Ehmet could see the driver staring at the roadway, not seeming to notice the surrounding country-side. Whoever was driving looked to be alone and intent on get-ting wherever he was going quickly. Ehmet wondered whether the driver was indeed headed toward the city with messages, arms, goods to sell, or to try to find someone there. If he was a smuggler from one of the gangs, he would have had passage arranged, bought, and paid for. But if he was just someone travel-ing on his own, as the father of one of Ehmet's friends had done, the whole trip would be one of greater dangers and risk. Only the best planning, the quickest responses to danger, and a large dose of luck could aid the solo traveler. Ehmet's friend's father had been working in France when the fighting started. By using a French passport, which didn't identify him as someone from here, and therefore not the potential enemy of someone else from here, he had managed to drive from Paris to Sarajevo to get back to his family. He had faced roadblocks, veered through torn-up roads, exploding mines, and gunfire; had talked and paid and snuck his way by gangs and soldiers, each of whom identified "the enemy" as someone "different" from themselves—and somehow arrived, his family thought miraculously, in Sarajevo.

Ehmet resolved to be careful, to try to think things out and act in ways that would make his, and his mother's, journey successful. He realized again how difficult that might be when, as he neared the barn on his return, he heard several explosions, not too distant. Mines, he thought, and wondered what had happened to the driver he had just seen. He pictured another family waiting in Sarajevo, wondering, too.

Inside the barn, his mother still slept. Ehmet sat down in the hay near her and ate several of the apples he had brought. Even if their exteriors were a bit uneven, the apples were delicious. He could make a meal of apples—first, second, third course, and dessert—a regular feast. He peered into the pocket of hay at his mother's face. She did not seem to have stirred yet. He decided to go back into the field and dig potatoes from the plant he had seen. They would need to be cooked to be eaten. He didn't want to make a fire here, but they could be carried in his backpack for later. He found what was left of an old, rusted, shovel blade still attached to a small piece of its wooden handle. To someone else it had probably seemed like useless junk, but to Ehmet it was just what was needed.

We need that, he laughed to himself. "We need that" was a family joke from a weekend camping trip by the sea last summer, before all this had started, when the world was a place where vacations, trips for pleasure, could take place. Ehmet had said "We need that," as he picked up a rubber band he spied on the ground. He had always picked up things that seemed worthless to almost everyone else.

"We need that?" his father had teased.

"Well, we might," Ehmet had said.

They had enjoyed the afternoon walking the beach. Ehmet examined unusual rocks and odd sticks, and added a few notable ones to the collection in his pockets. Later in the day, after they had cooked dinner, Ehmet's mother was trying to seal a plastic bag that had noodles left in it. There was no obvious way to close it and not enough left to tie the top into a knot. Ehmet had reached into his pocket and pulled out the rubber band.

"Here," he had said.

She looked at it curiously for a moment, then as she took the band and wrapped it around the bag to seal it, she had said with a big smile, "We need that!"

"Yes," his father had agreed, "we do need that!"

In recent months, a lot more unusual things had suddenly seemed useful, and when someone picked up something or brought it home, the family still joked "We need that."

Ehmet definitely needed, could use, the old shovel. He picked it up and headed to the field again. He paused just outside the barn door. The tractor was no longer running. There was no other noise except a bird warbling, and no people visible. Ehmet bent low again just in case and made his way to the potato plant. The earth was packed hard, the field hadn't been plowed for a long time. The old shovel blade bent, yet still served its purpose. As he forced it into the ground with his foot, he was able to break loose chunks of earth around the base of the potato plant. When he had dug to the depth where he thought the potatoes should be, he reached into the small hole and felt around in the loose dirt. No potatoes. In the past he might have given up at this point. But as much as he liked apples, the potatoes were the only other food readily available, and the idea of having some pushed him and the shovel on.

He deepened and broadened the hole, and as he reached around this time he felt potatoes. Small ones. This was not his grandparent's fertile garden where the carefully tended potatoes, easy to dig in their loose earth, grew the size of grapefruits. These were potatoes nonetheless, and Ehmet gathered all he could find, a few handfuls, and dropped them into the same makeshift, sweatshirt bag he had used for the apples.

Back in the barn, he added the potatoes to his backpack. He went over and sat in the hay by his sleeping mother to wait for her to awake. Before he had time to think about it, he had fallen asleep.

◇

SEVEN

The Awakening

When Ehmet awoke, it was to find a hand on his shoulder. Instinctively, he pulled away from the hand, then remembered that he had been waiting and watching over his mother and awakened more fully to find her seated next to him.

"Sorry," she said as Ehmet's eyes focused in the still-dark barn.

"I didn't know it was you. I thought it might be somebody . . . " Tears collected in her eyes, and he stopped talking.

"Sorry," she said again.

"It's all right, Mom."

Her eyes overflowed and she wiped her face with the sleeve of the fleece shirt he had given her to change into.

"Grandma and Granddad's," she said in a low voice, "we'll go to Grandma and Granddad's."

Ehmet had never seen his mother like this. He wanted to know why, but knew he couldn't ask now.

Going to his grandmother and grandfather's house seemed like a good idea. They lived far on the other side of the mountains, in Croatia, in an area where there had been no fighting. His grandparents' house was in the countryside. Many of his own country experiences had been with them, and much of what he knew of country life came from what they had shown him and their stories. Something his mother had often said, "You always have your family," now rang in his mind like the persistent clanging of one of the coastal bells that sounded to guide ships at sea through night, fog, or storms.

"How?" Ehmet asked.

"However we can," said his mother. "Come on."

"Now?"

"No one will see us in the dark."

He peered outside. Stars shown, and the partial moon lit the edges of scattered clouds as they passed. It must have been the middle of the night. Ehmet thought that he had slept awhile, though he was still tired. This was the second night that was mostly not sleep. He wondered what time it was, and looked to his mother's wrist for her familiar watch. It wasn't there. He was about to ask her what time it was, thinking the watch must be in a pocket, when he noticed that her wedding ring was no longer on her finger. The ring she always wore. And she had no earrings on, either. He realized that these things being missing had to do with what had happened last night. He asked nothing.

Ehmet dug into the outside pocket of his backpack. He had put his watch there yesterday, before he went to play soccer. Now kicking the ball around with friends was a distant and out of place memory, so much had crashed into his life since then. His hand found the watch in the dark pocket. His parents had given it to him last year. By pressing a couple of buttons on the side it could be used as a stopwatch, too. Another button made the watch face light up. He pushed it and held up the watch. It was three fifteen in the morning. He let the button go. The light went out, and they were in the dark again.

His mother was standing by the barn door, waiting for him. He thought she was studying the fields outside.

He reached next to him and grabbed his backpack, and climbed into the loft to retrieve the clothes he'd left there to dry.

When he slung the pack back on, it felt much heavier than it had before. A couple of lumps poked into his back. The potatoes and apples, he thought. He took the pack off for a moment and pulled out an apple before he strapped the pack on again.

"Here, Mom," he said, trying to hand her the apple. She stared at it. "You aren't hungry?" She shook her head. "You should eat something." He knew she had not eaten since yesterday. "I just got these from the tree, they're good."

She accepted the apple slowly and took a bite. She chewed, but as she started to swallow, she doubled over and vomited.

She straightened up. "I'll have it later." She stuck the apple into the pocket of the fleece shirt she was wearing and moved no farther, gazing into the field. Ehmet saw that she was staring absently, drifting into the night. She did not seem to see even him. Whatever they were going to do, for the moment he would have to lead. He sprang fully awake.

EIGHT

◇

Bobbing and Weaving

To start off, Ehmet thought that following the road near the barn would be best. If they stayed near the road, he was sure that they would be headed in the right direction. They would not go in the direction of the car that Ehmet had seen and wondered about that morning. They would travel the opposite way, away from Sarajevo. Ehmet had a good sense of direction. His father and mother had noticed this when he was three years old and they were driving near a park they often visited. As they drove past a corner where they usually turned, from the backseat his small voice piped, "Turn."

"What?" his father had questioned.

"Turn!" he had piped again.

"That's the way to the park," said his mother. "He wants to go to the park!"

From then on, his parents had made a game of asking him how to get places. They would tell him what place they were trying to go to, and along the way ask him how to get there. "Turn!" or "Straight!" he would call out.

As he got older they made the game harder by trying routes they had not taken before, and he could almost always find the way. That ability had served him well in the past months as he tried to find new, safer routes through the city. No matter how many twists or turns he took through alleys and backyards, around buildings or even ducking through drainpipes or abandoned water tunnels, he had only gotten lost twice. Each of those times, finding himself in places he did not recognize, he had stopped, oriented himself and, after a little wandering, found his direction. Once he had turned the corner of an alleyway in a part of the city he did not know well to find himself facing a roadblock in the street. It was manned by a heavily armed gang, submachine guns in hands, pistols in their belts. Fortunately, the thugs had been busy harassing the driver of a car. Ehmet sprang to turn, and ran, retracing the way he had come. When someone yelled "Stop!" from behind him, he had not looked back. And he had not mentioned that incident to his parents—they were worried enough whenever he went out.

Now he was worried about his mother. He took her hand and led the way. As they left the barn she walked hurriedly. But she slowed after the first few steps as they crossed the field to reach the bridge. Ehmet was a fast walker. When walking with other people he often got ahead of them, and they asked him to slow down. He was used to that. His mother, though, was not asking him. She had simply slowed so that he was now pulling at her arm. He turned, and saw that she was hobbling and grimacing. When she walked, she was obviously in pain.

"Mom?"

"Keep going. Walk as fast as we can."

He slowed his pace immediately. There was plenty to watch for anyway, and they had a long way to go. They would have to walk at a pace that was comfortable for his mother. Ehmet started to calculate how long it might take them to reach his grandparents' house. This was like the kind of math problem his teacher had given them in class. "If a car travels at an average of fifty miles an hour and takes nine hours to reach its destination, how long would it take someone walking at the speed of . . . "

Last summer, when he and his parents had taken a camping trip, walking with backpacks in the mountains, they had tried to figure out how fast they were walking by looking at the map to see what distance they had covered, and how long it took them. His mother had figured their speed was about three miles an hour. There had been a lot of walking up and down over rough country, and they had heavy backpacks on that trip. Now they didn't have the big backpacks to carry, and it shouldn't be as rough if they traveled along the roads. Ehmet hoped that would balance out the difficulty his mother was having in walking. Besides, she would probably start to feel better. He decided that two and a half miles an hour was a reasonable number to use.

When Ehmet had traveled by car to his grandparents' house from Sarajevo, it had taken nine hours on the winding roads. Here they were what would have been about an hour's normal drive outside Sarajevo. "So, walking two and a half miles an hour, that's about one-twentieth the speed of the car. It would take twenty times as long walking as driving the rest of the way. So one hundred and sixty hours," he calculated to himself. "One hundred sixty hours' walking, one hundred sixty hours' walking . . . how many days would that be?" That depended on how many hours they could walk per day, or night. There were too many variables to figure it out easily. It could be a few weeks. Weeks? No, he didn't think so. Either way, they had started, and they were walking.

By the time Ehmet had finished his attempts to calculate their trip they had reached the bridge. Looking both ways, he again considered getting help from some of his friends. Maybe someone would even be able to give them a ride part way.

"Mom, maybe we could get help from Ivan's family, or . . . "

"Got to get out of here now," said his mother emphatically. "Don't know where they've gone."

By "they," Ehmet was fairly certain that she meant those from last night. Though if she meant Ivan's family, it was true that something similar to last night could have happened to them. Ehmet worried too about Boda and Petar. But it was clear from his mother's limited words and tone that she did not want more discussion.

Ehmet strained to hear any vehicles. He heard none, so they started across the river on the old span. There were stone walls lining both edges of the narrow bridge, nowhere to hide if a vehicle did come along. Ehmet and his mother would be caught standing by the path of any passing vehicle. Ehmet felt far too exposed, and expected to hear a vehicle roar up at any moment. His heart thudded hard against his chest. He could not rely on the kindness or neutrality of passersby, and he vowed to stay hidden as much as possible on their journey. The wisdom of his mother's idea to travel tonight became clearer: They were much less likely to be seen. Their feet might stumble on bumps in dark paths, but there were greater obstacles, mainly the type that could speak or yell or careen along in machines.

Crossing the bridge without incident was enough of an accomplishment to bring some release to Ehmet. He led his mother farther, along the margins of the roadway where they could easily duck into a field or forest should a vehicle appear. He looked around for Luci. The last time he had seen her was around the barn. What might happen to her? She was a hunter though, and he had seen her find her way home from greater distances. Cats were territorial. Probably she had gone back to Uncle Petar and Aunt Boda's farm to reclaim it, whether they were there or not. He shuddered, and wondered if she would still find it home.

For the first hour of so of their travel Ehmet was nervous, walking stiffly, constantly tuned for unexpected sound or for someone to leap at him in the dark. Then he found that he was relaxing into a moving rhythm. Before, he had not walked for any great length of time in unlit night. It had its own hypnotic effect.

His mother stumbled, and he caught her on his arm before she fell to the ground. He had caught his foot, too, on a root or a stone a number of times; it was easy to do on the dark shoulders of the road. He kept remembering to keep his pace slow, so they were able to walk together. He wondered aloud if she needed to stop walking.

"No," she said, "let's get as far as we can." Beyond that, she was still not talkative. Her face was set in a steady gaze. To Ehmet, she was someone who talked and laughed easily most of the time. When she was ready, Ehmet thought, she would say more.

They walked until Ehmet could see the slightest lightening of the sky above the trees and hills. They would have to find someplace to rest soon if they were to wait out the day in hiding. Along the way they had passed numerous fields, scattered houses, and barns. When they had come near a village, Ehmet had avoided the road that entered it. As they skirted the village, a dog in the yard of one of the houses barked wildly and alarmed both Ehmet and his mother, and apparently the owners of the house. A light had flicked on inside, and Ehmet and his mother hurried away.

Ehmet looked for another abandoned house or barn. The closest looked tended and likely to be currently used, with tools standing against the outside walls. The sky was rapidly brightening toward day. A car sputtered down the road from the direction of the village they had passed. Ehmet pulled his mother down into the high grasses that lined the roadway and the two of them ducked out of sight. The car did not stop. *Good,* thought Ehmet. *They either didn't see us or don't care who we are.* He waited until the sound of the car had disappeared, poked his head up, and periscope-like turned in a full circle to study all directions. He spied what appeared to be an abandoned shed at the far edge of the field next to them.

They started through the border of bushes that edged the field. Brambles pulled at their clothes. They bobbed and weaved between scratchy branches as best they could. Several times Ehmet had to unhook their snagged pant legs and sleeves from thorned bushes. When they entered the bramble-free field Ehmet was relieved. He guided them through the swaying, high grass to the shed.

Inside, it was dusty and smelled of farm animals. Straw was heaped in a corner and empty cloth feed and seed sacks were strewn about. Ehmet gathered several of the sacks and laid them out over a bit of the straw to make a mattress. His mother needed no encouragement to lie down there, and without saying a word fell immediately to sleep. He placed a couple more empty bags over her as a blanket, then made a similar mattress for himself. He piled straw around so they would not be so easily seen, then pulled bags and as much straw as he could over himself to cover. On the soft bed, Ehmet was fairly comfortable physically, but was still too uneasy to sleep. He tugged his backpack close to his head, looped a hand through the straps, and peered at a crack in the board wall of the shed. The stripe of bright daylight was the last thing he remembered.

NINE

The Desert

Ehmet awoke in a sweat and bolted into a sitting position. He had been dreaming about walking in a desert night, bobbing along with a flashlight, on guard for sharp beads of light reflected from snakes' eyes. Instead, he found himself sitting on the mattress of sacks and straw. His mother sat near him awake, studying him.

"You were sweating."

Ehmet was getting used to sweating. "I was dreaming."

"About what?"

"A desert." His mother waited. Ehmet said nothing more. He tried to forget the dream for now. He felt that talking about the snakes could add fears to those already hissing in the air.

"A desert would at least be warm. Teenagers sweat more. Are you ready for that?"

Ehmet was not sure what he was ready for. He looked outside. It was dark. He must have slept through the day. His watch showed that it was nine thirty.

"I slept most of the day, too," said his mother. "But I woke up a few times."

"What are we going to do?" Ehmet asked.

"Walk," his mother said. "Keep doing the best we can. It looks as if you've been busy. I saw the potatoes in your backpack." Normally Ehmet would have been offended that she had gone through his backpack. She usually left his belongings alone. But it was no longer his pack anyway. They were sharing it, and what little it contained.

"I was putting your shirt back," she said, acknowledging too the change in their ways. Ehmet noticed that she had changed into her own sweater. She was still wearing his extra pair of pants though, rather than the torn skirt she had had on when she arrived at the tree from Aunt Boda and Uncle Petar's. Ehmet was tempted again to ask about them, then thought better of it. His mother was just starting to sound a bit like her usual self.

"Aren't you hungry?" he asked instead. She had eaten almost nothing these last couple of days.

"Yes. But not for raw potatoes." She coughed, and wiped her hair away from her eyes with the back of her hand.

"There are some more apples at the bottom of the backpack. We could cook the potatoes later." He reached into the pack and dug until he found an apple. When she had eaten it, he gave her another.

"That's better," she said. "Are you ready to go?"

"I guess."

"Walking at night we can stay hidden. I want to be hidden."

Ehmet agreed. He wanted to use a flashlight like in his dream to light the path, not searching for snakes but to illuminate the dangers they might face here. A small, beady-eyed snake would be a relief compared to the much larger things they could run into walking these paths. And the two-footed creatures would not stop frozen by light in their eyes. The light for them could be a beacon, a flashing sign advertising Ehmet's and his mother's presence. So Ehmet and his mother again set out walking, in the dark.

TEN

Ruins

The only sounds the two of them made besides the faint scuffing of their feet and crunching of occasional leaves or twigs were his mother's coughs. She tried to stifle them, but they were rasping forth more often in a ragged staccato. Ehmet worried that someone would hear.

The moon that had been a sliver a few days ago was growing slowly in size and in the amount of light it provided. Yet it was still difficult to avoid stumbling, being scratched by brambles, or getting whacked by branches. There were very few vehicles on the roads at night, and so far the greatest difficulties were in avoiding farmhouses and villages, people, barking dogs, and places Ehmet thought likely to have landmines—by the entrances to settlements for example. The road they were following was headed in the right direction as far as Ehmet could tell. When it was necessary to leave the roadway they walked parallel to it in nearby forests or fields so that they could continue to follow its route. Ehmet kept the North Star on his right so they continued generally west. He wanted a map. That would give them additional clues they needed to make their way as directly as possible. They could use a map.

Several times they had passed houses closely enough to see evidence of attacks—jagged, gaping holes from explosives, walls pockmarked with craters left by bullets—the burned out, scorched shells of what had once been homes. They had moved carefully by those buildings as they had those that looked occupied, trying to avoid any contact with the unknown, though Ehmet was becoming more willing to venture closer. The buildings themselves might hold supplies they needed. He decided to enter the next abandoned building that he could get into on his own.

It wasn't long before he had the opportunity. Close to the changing light of dawn, they wearily came near a village. It was clear the place had recently been attacked since some of the buildings were still smoldering. Piercing orange, ember eyes glowed from the skeletons of houses, barns, and a shop or two. Trails of smoke snaked into the dim light.

Ehmet's mother moved away from the destruction. She sped her pace and with shaky legs appeared ready to run, though both she and Ehmet were exhausted from their night of walking. They veered in a wide arc around buildings, keeping to the treed outskirts of the village. Birdsongs that would normally be heard in the dawn were replaced by an unnerving silence. Animals had their own ways of acknowledging war. A dog began to bark and continued unceasingly. Ehmet watched for people and movement. They heard no gunfire, yet whoever had attacked here might still be close by.

As they skirted around the village, Ehmet glimpsed clothes and other household contents—pans, furniture—strewn outside buildings. His mother hurried on. When they had passed the farthermost edge of this unsettled settlement, they came upon an isolated ruin in a semi-cleared space in the forest. The building had obviously been abandoned for many years. Where parts of the stone walls had collapsed in heaps, plants grew from among the ancient rocks. A few hand-hewn beams supported what was left of a tile roof, and an ancient, broken, two-wheeled horse cart sat out of the weather in the shadows below. Ehmet scouted around. There would not be any particular attraction here for people passing, but the remaining walls and roof would provide some shelter.

He led his mother inside to a dim corner of their refuge. Passing the destroyed village had shoved her back into grim wordlessness. She pulled off her shoes and socks and Ehmet saw popping red blisters where her feet had rubbed against her shoes. His own feet were sore. He had been used to walking, but walking for so many hours, nights, over uneven terrain, stumbling over rocks and roots, was taking a toll. Besides the bruises, there was the tension with each lifted step that when a foot returned to the ground it might land on a mine and disappear in bone-shattering explosion. This unnerving idea Ehmet had been able to keep at bay for periods of time, and with the passing steps he had reassured himself that they might somehow evade mines. He pulled off his shoes and socks and looked at his reddened and raw feet. So far he only had one blister. His soft running shoes were better for walking than the leather shoes his mother had been wearing. She lay down on the earthen floor, curled herself into a ball, and closed her eyes.

The cool, hard-packed earth felt good on Ehmet's bare feet. He doubted though that it was a good surface for his mother to sleep on. The cool damp might worsen her cough. Today her hacking had been more ferocious and frequent.

"It's only a cold," his mother had kept insisting.

Ehmet had an idea for a soothing remedy, yet it would take some time to prepare. Now he wanted to get her settled more comfortably.

The inside of the crumbling building had long ago been stripped of signs of the lives it had once contained. Only the big cart remained, with wheels taller than Ehmet, iron rims arched above his head. He climbed up on the wooden spokes of one wheel and looked into the flat bottom of the cart box. The wooden planks of the cart floor were worn smooth from many years of sliding loads, whatever it may have hauled. Ehmet sniffed—no musty odors of dung. It was amazingly clean.

Ehmet climbed back down. "Mom."

She didn't stir. He leaned to nudge her, then did not, remembering how she had reacted recently. "Mom," he repeated louder.

Her eyelids peeped halfway open. She shivered, tucked herself into a tighter ball, recoiled, and squinted, only then seeming to see that it was Ehmet.

"Mom, there's a better place to sleep."

She opened her eyes more fully, not moving otherwise. Ehmet extended his hand. She took it. He gently pulled her to a standing position. She held his arm as he helped her to climb the wheel to get into the cart. Once she was in the cart box, she immediately lay down again. Ehmet climbed down to retrieve the backpack. When he was standing on the floor, his mother could not be seen at all. The high sides of the cart box hid her.

He picked up the backpack and his mother's shoes and socks and hauled the lot up into the cart box. His mother was already asleep. Ehmet took almost everything out of the pack, wadded the clothes into a ball as a pillow that he eased next to her head, and piled harder things like the potatoes he had gathered, the two apples that remained, the flashlight, the notebook, and Milan's book in a corner of the cart. Maybe he would read today. He picked the book up and examined the blurb on the back: *"This is a story about the invasion of the Alien Cashews. Cashews are not nuts. Cashews are seeds, even if alien."* One of the oddest story summaries he had read. Ehmet had other things to do at the moment.

His mother seemed relatively safe here. He slung the pack, empty except for the water bottle, onto his back, climbed down to the floor and gathered his shoes and socks. He gently massaged his raw feet and left them bare to enjoy the cool floor as he walked outside.

First he wanted to work on the remedy for his mother's cough. He scoured the meadow for plants that might be useful, ones he remembered from his grandparents' lessons. Among the grasses he spotted the teardrop-shaped leaves of a plantain plant. His grandparents had crushed the leaves and put it on his irritated skin several times. It might cool the blisters on his mother's feet.

When he found the white, fuzzy leaves of a mullein plant, good for coughs if brewed into tea, Ehmet was jubilant. At the edge of the meadow he gathered some wild berry-plant leaves to add to the brew. The problem was, besides not wanting to build a fire that might attract attention, Ehmet had no pot in which to boil water. But a plan was simmering.

Near their skeletal shelter a brook wandered by, water not in a hurry downhill. It must have flowed strong at times of the year when there was more rain, and from snowmelt in spring, since the stones along the waterside were rounded and worn smooth. The water was invitingly clear. Ehmet so far had kept to his resolution not to drink from such open, flowing waters they'd encountered, because of the waste and microscopic critters that could be picked up as the water traveled near people or animals. He thought that resolve had probably saved him so far from stomachaches. Searching along the brook, he found a rivulet of water trickling in over one bank. Following the trickle back from the brook, Ehmet spied a small pool tucked between rocks. Crystal clear water bubbled from the bottom of the mossy pool, filtered directly out of the earth. Ehmet scooped handfuls of the sparkling water to his mouth. It was icy and refreshing, clean tasting with its own sweetness.

He took the water bottle out of his pack, filled it, and walked back to the ruins. Ehmet crushed mullein and berry-plant leaves and stuffed them into the bottle. Then he set the bottle in the sunlight, propped among some rocks so as to reflect even more of the heat to cook the brew. Sun tea.

He returned to the brook, found a boulder to sit on, and dipped his feet into the dark pool that collected below it. The water was shockingly frigid. It started cold from the spring, and fall days and cooler nights had lowered its temperature further. His feet quickly became numb. Numbness was a pleasant change from pain, yet it was disconcerting not to feel his feet. He pulled them from the water. They were white from cold, then surged red from within as his blood rushed to warm them. He rested them on the sun-warmed curve of the boulder and turned his head up to the sky.

To feel the sun's warmth was a pleasure. The nights of walking had been quiet and cold. He basked in the sun, letting it burn away the lingering chill.

A snapping twig popped Ehmet out of his turtlelike basking. His eyes sprang open and he swiveled to look where he had heard the sound. A squirrel pulled an acorn from a twig, let the twig drop, and scurried away with the prized food held securely in its mouth. Ehmet's stomach knocked twice. He was hungry. Acorns might be a sumptuous treat for a squirrel, but as far as Ehmet knew, were bitter to humans. Just to make sure that these were like the acorns he had tried a bite of once or twice when he was younger, Ehmet picked one up and eased his teeth through the leathery shell. Mouth-puckering bitter.

The brook held food promise—clear and moving, with rocky pools. Ehmet hoped trout hid here. If so, he thought he could find them. He had learned to see fish when he started fly fishing two years ago.

He squatted on the edge of the brook, waiting. Soon he saw the shadow of a fish, not easily distinguished from the flickering underwater shapes of the rocky bottom. Instantly he swooped his hand bearlike into the water to scoop up the darting form. Apparently he didn't have the paws for it. He came up with only a dripping hand.

He tried another technique in a pool farther down the creek. Lying facedown, draped over a boulder, he dangled an arm in the water and held his hand still on the rocky bottom, palm up. He had tried this on other occasions, and found that leaving his hand motionless, the fish either didn't notice it or were curious and swam close to investigate. Sure enough, when his hand had been in the water long enough to start to numb, a fish swam over it. As he closed his hand he felt a swirl of smooth fish skin slipping away.

So much for hands-on approaches. It was time to make fishing tools. He took out the fishing line he'd stashed in his pocket days ago, untangled it, and tied on the thorn he'd collected as a makeshift hook. Turning over a log near the brook, he turned up several wriggling, juicy gray grubs for bait.

Dangling the rig into a pool, he got a strike and tugged the line toward him. Bare thorn hung at the end of the line. The grub was gone and so was the fish. He rigged and tried again several times. The fish easily stole the bait without getting hooked. Ehmet had wondered if a thorn would really work. He'd seen something like it in a book illustration about ancient fishing tools. If it had ever worked, it would take a lot more practice and probably longer than his stomach would hold out.

He put on his shoes and socks, went to check on his mother, and set off again with the almost weightless, empty backpack dangling from his shoulders.

ELEVEN

Who?

It was not far back to the village. Though the day was not that warm, Ehmet sweated nervously. He stopped and tipped his head slowly first toward one shoulder then the other. His neck crackled with small pangs of pain then relief when bones shifted into more comfortable positions. He had plenty of other aches from all the walking and holding himself in tense alert.

When he reached the edge of the village he thought about turning back. The fire-scorched and shattered walls told the full-blown ferocity of the destruction that had taken place here. As he got closer, Ehmet could make out the distinctive pockmarks of bullets, and larger holes from mortars or heavy shells and rockets. Clothes, toys, pots, and pans were scattered in yards and across streets. The smoldering buildings sent puffs of smoke that hung in the air like the small, white clouds of his breath in the cold of early morning. He breathed hard. The day had warmed. He could no longer see his breath.

Ehmet looked across the field that spread out between him

and the nearest shell of a building. The field was well tended, not full of weeds like many he had seen. Someone had recently cut the hay from it, which lay in piles dotting the field. He strained to hear sounds other than his own breathing. He heard none of the thumping, clattering of tools, vehicle noises, or voices that come with the beginning of a day in a village. All he heard was his own body.

"Listen to your own voice," his father had often told him. He knew what his father meant, to have faith in his own ideas.

"Hello," he whispered to himself. He laughed. This was the first time lately that he had thought of his father without being upset or angry at him for sending him and his mother away. . . . Ehmet avoided climbing aboard that slogging train for the moment and returned his focus to the village and what he might find of use there. He had been avoiding people, houses, and the dangers that the unknown might present. He had been orbiting around the unknown like a moon around an unnamed planet for long enough. Ehmet wanted to know what was on this planet, in this place. Whether it was most important to know, make some kind of contact, or find useful things, he could not have said. He was simply circling closer, and instincts he had to flee were overcome by the gravitylike pull.

Instead of the most direct route in, crossing the open hay field, he jogged along a stone wall at its edge. The stones had been cleared from the field over the years, probably over thousands of years, and piled on the wall by the farmers who had lived here. This was not a newly inhabited part of Earth. Most recently it had been called Bosnia, before that Yugoslavia, before that it had had many different names and many different people who had claimed it. The history Ehmet had read and heard about was not of days, or weeks, or years, or even centuries, but of thousands of years. In other times, Ehmet would have stopped to search the field for relics turned upward with the earth. Once, in a newly plowed field, he had spotted a Roman coin, two thousand years old. Its rough, rounded shape with an ancient, curlyhaired and wreathed head depicted on it had led his imagination sliding into a past with creaking wooden wheels of a merchant's cart and oxen pulling a tree-branch plow across the field. Now he glanced at this field mostly to avoid tripping as he ran.

The first house that he arrived at was entirely burned, the interior walls charred and roofless. He could see little inside that was recognizable for what it had been, just burnt remnants, charcoaled angles, and curls of black and white. A refrigerator had survived intact with a paint-blistered, bubbling skin. Only the stove stood strangely gleaming, since it was built to take heat.

Belongings weren't scattered in the yard. This house appeared to have burned with all that it contained inside. Looted houses usually had signs of plunder strewn around them, bits torn from within and abandoned outside like when a dog tips over a trash can, takes only the choicest bits, and leaves the rest scattered where it falls.

Ehmet ventured on, scouting around the corner of the burned house before dashing down the lane to the next. This second house was more intact; it had been battered but not burned. In the yard among clothes were a stuffed toy bear and a radio with a cracked plastic casing, smashed into the mud. A family's belongings were now litter. Ehmet felt exposed. He strained to hear any sound that he could associate with people, sounds he hoped for and at the same time feared. Nothing. The hairs on the back of his neck bristled. To hear nothing in a place that would ordinarily be filled with sounds was eerie. Ehmet darted into the house through the open, front door.

Once inside he peeked out of the doorway to reassure himself. No one appeared.

He squinted back into the dark interior of the house. As his eyes adjusted, he could see a couch, a tipped over chair, a few clothes scattered around the room. Whoever had been here had been frenzied. Drawers were pulled open, pictures on the walls turned at odd angles. He walked over to a photograph and instinctively straightened it as he looked more closely. It appeared to be a family with a few children, one a boy probably a bit younger than Ehmet, and two smaller children. Ehmet was uneasy, this was someone else's place. Yet there was some comfort just being in a home. Ehmet missed having a bed to sleep in and a floor on which he could drop his running shoes. He sat on the couch.

There was no use dallying. Ehmet mentally remade the list of the things he and his mother needed and could use. Food was at the top of the list, any kind of food, and a pot for cooking the potatoes he had been carrying in his backpack. A blanket. The fall nights, even many of the days, were cold. Matches had been on the list. Seeing the smoldering fires around the village he figured he could carry a bit of fire, a piece of embered wood, with him if he had to, like some prehistoric runner wrapped in an animal skin, carrying the flame, careful to keep it away from his flammable robe. Still, matches would be easier. Batteries, too. Electrical power in a little capsule, battery-style—a big change from cave days. He could drop batteries into his flashlight and poof, cut a path of light through the night. Mighty sword of light, galactic conqueror, "Look out, Darth Vader!"

Back on planet Earth Ehmet spotted a jacket on the floor, a windbreaker with a fuzzy lining that would be handy. He put it on and checked the roomy side pockets. His fingers found a small box with sandpaper on one side. Matches. He shook the box without taking it out of the pocket. Matches rattled around inside. This was good. One item on the list. Ehmet was encouraged. He decided to check the kitchen next.

The doors of the cupboards had been left open. Dishes and broken jars littered the countertop. In an open drawer next to the sink, he spied a few utensils. He took out a couple of forks and several large spoons and stuck them into the inside pocket of the jacket he had adopted.

Little remained in the cupboards, but Ehmet figured that he had the best chance of finding food there, something that had been overlooked or that someone else had decided was not worth the trouble to take. He righted a knocked-over chair and pulled it to the counter. Standing on it he could examine what was left on the lower shelves—a few dishes, an upended glass flower vase, a couple of dented cooking pots. He picked out a light, aluminum saucepan with a handle and set it on the counter. By climbing on the counter among the rubble, he could reach into the highest shelves. He could not see up there so was guided by touch. He groped around the front of the topmost shelf and didn't encounter anything. Uncertainly he slid his hand farther into the unknown at the back of the shelf.

A can! A flat, rectangular one. He grasped it and slid it toward him. Something ran across his hand, tiny sharp claws flicking over his skin. He recoiled and jerked his hand out of the cupboard. The can slipped from his grip and thumped onto the counter as he lost his balance and tumbled backward.

The chair he had climbed up on broke his fall. He found himself draped over it with the breath knocked out of him, the side of the chair poking into his stomach. Ehmet inhaled and felt his body. A few pangs and dings from the fall. Basically he seemed okay. He was about to try to stand up when he heard a noise from the cupboard under the sink, now near his head. His first thought was that it was the rodent or whatever it was that had run across his hand. How had it gotten down here so quickly? And the noise was not the kind of scratching noise that a small animal would make. This had the hollow sound of something larger, thumping against the wooden cabinet from within.

Ehmet crouched, and pulled the cabinet door open quickly. In the shadows under the sink was a heap of clothes, maybe rags, Ehmet thought. Then he saw a leg sticking out of the pile, a small bare leg with a sock and a child-size worn leather shoe on the foot. He slowly reached out to touch it.

"Nooo!" a voice screamed sharply as the leg burrowed under the pile of cloth. The huge sound crashed through the room and any illusions Ehmet had of being alone.

"It's me," said Ehmet quietly when the scream finally stopped.

There was no response. "It is just me," he repeated a little louder.

Again, for a few moments, there was no response. Then a child's voice asked, "Who?"

◇

TWELVE

Not Alone

Ehmet then realized that "me" was probably not enough information to comfort whoever was under the clothes. "Ehmet" wouldn't be of much use to a kid he didn't know either. He wondered if "Tarzan" or "Luke Skywalker" would be any better.

"I'm just another kid. I won't hurt you."

Hands from within pushed some of the pile of cloth away. A boy's face appeared, a face that looked familiar to Ehmet. It was the boy from the photograph in the living room. Ehmet guessed the boy was around ten or eleven years old.

"Who are you?" the boy asked Ehmet, tears streaming down his cheeks.

"Ehmet."

"I mean who are you?"

Ehmet was not sure what to say. How do you tell someone who you are?

"What are you doing here? You're not with them, are you?"

"Them?" Ehmet asked.

"The guys who were here . . . "

"I came by myself," Ehmet said.

"So you're not with them?"

"Who?"

"The men. With guns." The boy tried to wipe away tears. "Took my family away. I was at my friend's house and I heard shooting. I ran back here. When I was almost home I could see them pushing my parents into the back of a truck. It drove away before I could catch up." The boy's crying overtook his talking and did not appear likely to stop soon. Ehmet realized that he himself had not cried for some time, had not allowed himself to feel the force of the torrent that the boy was caught in, although this sobbing was inviting Ehmet to think about taking a dip. He turned away.

The boy's shaking sobs turned to stuttered breathing. Ehmet thought he could be heard now. "When were they here?" he asked, partly to get an idea of the potential danger. He had hoped from the silence that whoever had attacked the village was gone.

"Two . . . two days ago," the boy said, catching his breath.

Ehmet had fleeting shadowy images of bodies thrashing and thumping, accompanied by shouts and yells like he had heard at his aunt and uncle's farm.

The boy was watching him. "You could be one of them. You're big enough."

"I'm not. One of them."

"That looks like my father's jacket."

Ehmet wasn't sure what to say.

"That's my father's jacket, right? Why are you wearing his jacket?"

"I . . . I didn't think anyone was still here. I thought everyone had left, and everything here would just be sitting, or get taken by somebody else . . . "

"It's still our stuff."

"I know, I know. I'm sorry. Here." Ehmet took off the jacket and handed it to the boy.

The boy stood holding it and started to cry again. When he stopped, he looked around the room as if trying to find a place to put the jacket in the disarray.

He handed the jacket back to Ehmet. "You can borrow it. You can give it back to my father. If we leave it here, Chetniks will take it anyway. They'll try to get me, too."

Ehmet was becoming more and more uneasy about being in the village and in the boy's home.

"Somebody from your family will come and get you," Ehmet said, trying to comfort the boy.

"They won't! They can't."

"How do you know?"

"The men who took them were Serbs! Chetniks! They were saying for weeks they were going to get us. A Serb from our village even told us, 'We'll clear you out, you damn Muslims.' Damn Serbs! This is a Muslim village, our village. Not theirs."

Theirs, ours, us, them. Ehmet had heard those words so many times, as if all could be neatly divided. He was himself a mix of us's and thems.

"My family won't be able to come back," the boy repeated. "Not now."

"Is there someone you could stay with?"

"No. Almost everyone's gone. This is a Muslim village. Only a few Serbs lived here. I can't stay with them."

"What are you going to do?"

"Go somewhere. Leave. Serbs came yesterday. Two of them. I heard them coming into the house, so I hid. One of them said, 'This will be a good house for my family. We'll pack and move in. This will be a Serb village within the week.' The other said, 'We packed the Muslims out, now we can pack in!' They laughed. Pig Serbs! That's why I hid under the sink when you came. I thought you were them. You're not, are you?"

"I told you I wasn't."

"What are you then?"

Ehmet noticed the boy was now asking "what" he was rather than "who."

"Are you Muslim?" the boy pressed.

"My father is . . . Muslim, my mother is Croat Catholic. So what am I?"

The boy considered for a moment. "At least you're not Serb."

Ehmet could not see going further with his identity question. It was like being a pea under one of three shells in a shell game. Keep moving the shells around and guess which one has the pea under it. There were always lots of tricks with those games. It was hard to know what the right answer was, and if someone was trying to fool you.

"My family got chased out of my aunt and uncle's house by Serbs," Ehmet said. Yet it did not give him the particular sense of anger and satisfaction that the boy seemed to get from pinning it on the Serbs. Whoever could have done such things, some of which Ehmet did not want to imagine, had been violent and horrendous. On the streets of Sarajevo and in his journey since, Ehmet had seen that people with any name, of any group, could be smugglers, gang members, militia, thugs, preachers, or peacemakers. No group seemed to have a monopoly on doing harm or helping.

"I need to go," said Ehmet, edging from the kitchen into the living room.

"Alone?"

"My mother, too."

"Where is she?"

"Nearby."

"Can I go with you?" the boy begged.

Ehmet hesitated. "We're going to my grandparents' house in Croatia."

"I'll go . . . to my cousins'. You can just drop me off at my cousins' house. It's only about a day's walk. I know the way. It's on the way to Croatia." The boy pointed in what Ehmet thought was the right direction.

Ehmet was not anxious to have the boy along. He already had enough to contend with. But the boy was alone. Ehmet understood that.

The boy jumped into Ehmet's hesitation. "You're not from here. I know my way around. Besides, my cousins are nice. I'm sure they'll help you, too."

The boy was right. Ehmet was not from here. The prospects of having someone along who knew the land and of getting some help were appealing.

"Gather up whatever you want to take with you," said Ehmet. "You have a pack?"

"Yes."

"Be quick, okay? Is there any food here?"

"Not that I know of. But take things if you really need them. If you don't the Serbs, Chetniks, will. They take everything."

The boy scrambled into the hallway. Ehmet studied the room to see if there was anything that would be helpful. He found a blanket draped over the back of the couch, and rolled it up.

He went to the kitchen and retrieved the battered pot and the tin of sardines he had dropped on the counter. The boy must not have known about the sardines since they had been on the highest shelf, out of his reach. Ehmet wondered if other food might have been overlooked. He searched all of the cabinets and drawers. There was nothing else edible except salt in a glass shaker. He picked up an empty, plastic, water bottle. After placing his open mouth beneath the faucet to catch the luxurious clear stream of water, he filled the bottle, recapped it, and slid it into his backpack. Then he turned on the faucet again for a moment just to watch the sudden miracle of running water. He put the saltshaker, pot, sardines, and utensils into his pack.

"I'm ready." The boy was back, standing in the entryway to the kitchen. He had on a tattered, school backpack, stuffed so that bumps and bits stuck out.

Ehmet shouldered his pack. "Do you have what you want?" he asked the boy. As he said the words, he realized how out of place that question was. The boy had little of what he wanted. The quizzical look he gave Ehmet was his only answer.

"Warm clothes?"

"Yes."

Ehmet had another thought. "Do you have any fish hooks?"

The boy disappeared. Ehmet heard him rummaging in the next room. When he returned, he handed Ehmet a paper packet with several hooks.

"Great," said Ehmet. "Let's go."

THIRTEEN

◇

Burning

The boy knew where the ruins were. He didn't want to use the route Ehmet had taken to get into the village, by the open field. He said he could keep them more hidden. He led Ehmet along a path behind his house, passing close between other houses.

Smells of burning fogged the air. Broken glass from windows and chunks of walls and roofs littered the way. They hugged close to remaining walls and ducked below windows so they were not likely to be seen. They saw no one else, until glancing over a wooden fence into one backyard Ehmet spied a very old lady leaning over, tending her garden. Ehmet stopped to watch as she picked dead flowers off plants and brushed leaves clean of the powdery ash that had fallen on them from the burning, village air. She caressed buds, examining them for the blooms they might bring, not seeming to notice Ehmet and the boy nearby. She was absorbed in her garden. It was as if there was no war, no fighting, neither peace nor violence rippling the surface of time, she was immersed in a calmer, deeper pool of whatever always was, always had been.

The old lady's quiet actions were unusual in their usualness, and appeared bright if not brave acts in the moment. Ehmet was not accustomed to thinking of old ladies as brave. Sturdy, yes. He had been elbowed and poked out of the way by the sharp ends of umbrellas wielded by unstoppable old ladies on buses. This lady was courageous.

Ehmet was filled with new energy. He had been run down by the days of restless hiding and nights of walking. It had been like moving constantly into a storm wind. Suddenly he was buoyant, could float above the village and see himself and the boy running lightly and easily along the path.

When the path reached an alley that the boy whispered they would have to cross to continue, they paused to check it out. Peeking around the corner, Ehmet saw a car with bullet holes and broken windows, partly smashed and burned. Tracks of its tires led to where it now rested. It had been driven until recently, and might hold a few more things that could help on the way.

Ehmet's backpack had ceased to weigh on his back. He reached around to check that it was still there, and felt the lumps of what he was carrying.

"Wait here," he said to the boy.

"No!"

But the boy stayed where they had stopped on the path, tucked around the corner, as Ehmet ran down the alley to the car.

He ducked behind the car's trunk and pressed the button on the latch to release it. It clicked, and he pushed the trunk lid open. An oily rag and torn blanket lay in a heap. He pulled them aside. A large shiny tool for changing the tires was the only thing there.

He slid between the building wall and the side of the car to the front door. The door squeaked when he eased it open and climbed into the seat. The interior of the car had not burned much. When the car was set ablaze there had probably not been a lot of gas in the tank or engine. Ehmet thought of car trips he had taken with his family, packed lunches with stinky, boiled eggs he would now eat gladly, the radio on, tuning to new stations as they traveled from place to place, pulling the map from the glove box to see where they were going next.

The glove box was unlocked. There was as much treasure here as on any deserted isle—a scratched flashlight and a map. Ehmet flicked the switch of the flashlight. Nothing. Maybe just the bulb was burned out and the batteries were still good. He started to unfold the map. It was worn along the creases and smudged from the hands of many uses. It was a map of the places he needed. He could use it to find his way to Croatia. He was refolding it when he glimpsed movement through the windshield, farther up the alley.

Someone had been thrust headfirst out of a doorway, thrown into the muddy alley. Before Ehmet had a chance to figure out what was happening, two figures in marbled camouflage uniforms followed, poking rifle barrels at the man and yelling at him to get up.

Ehmet ducked below the dashboard and curled himself into the space where passengers would have put their feet. He wondered if he had been seen. He didn't think so. The uniformed men seemed preoccupied with the man they had been shoving along. He could hear yelling up the alley and felt his heart thumping at top speed.

Three shots popped. One sent little shards of glass raining down on Ehmet from the hole it created in what was left of the windshield.

"I saw something moving there!" someone down the alley yelled.

"It's nothing. You spend half your time shooting at nothing!"

Over his heartbeats Ehmet heard the voices receding. He waited until he could not hear anything, then waited in the silence some more. Finally he grabbed the steering wheel and hoisted himself up so that he could just see over the dashboard for an instant, and ducked back down as fast as he could. He closed his eyes to capture the image of what he had seen, like taking a picture, and now he was developing it. Empty alley. They had gone, he hoped. He slid over to the passenger door, eased it open and raced down the alley, back to the corner where he had left the boy. Ehmet almost knocked him over as he threw himself around the corner and onto the path. He twisted in midair to avoid the boy and fell in a heap next to him.

"I told you not to go out there," the boy said.

"I know."

"They were taking Mustafa. Who knows what they'll do with him. Kill him or make him work for them."

"They had masks," said Ehmet. Both of the armed men wore black, pullover masks that covered their heads, made them unidentifiable.

"Because they probably live around here. They don't want us to recognize them."

Not necessarily the greatest neighbors, thought Ehmet.

Ehmet peeked around the corner into the alley again. Clear. They rushed across to continue on the path out of the village. Sure-footed, the boy led them dodging through the village and into the surrounding forest without encountering anyone else. Once in the forest, they circled toward the ruins.

Ehmet rushed inside the old walls. Nothing appeared changed, the cart sat in the otherwise empty room as before. Ehmet climbed the wheel and looked over the edge of the cart side. His mother was not there.

Panic surged in Ehmet. He pivoted his head wildly searching the room—crumbling walls up to the roof beams, there was nowhere for his mother to be hidden. Ehmet's worst fear was that someone had found her, taken her away.

He breathed, breathed deep, and calmed enough to consider other possibilities. Perhaps she was outside. If he found her he would not let her out of his sight again.

Ehmet ran out of the building. He did not see his mother in the forest. He stumbled toward the brook.

There she sat, bathing her feet in the cool brook as he had done. She was in practically the same spot he had been. Maybe there was something to a gene pool, a thread that drew connected people to common elements.

She stood. "Hey." She waved, took a breath, and stifled a cough. "Who is this?" she said.

Ehmet turned to look where she was pointing. The boy. In his rush to look for his mother, he had forgotten the boy was there.

"It's . . . " He did not even know the boy's name.

"Ali," said the boy.

"I met him in the village."

"The village?" Ehmet's mother twisted her face in a disturbed grimace.

"We needed a few things. It's . . . it's okay." By "okay" he meant that he and the boy had escaped. He did not want to worry her with what he had encountered in the village.

Ali did not say everything was okay. "They took my family."

"Took . . . " said Ehmet's mother.

"Took them in a truck. Chetniks did."

"He'll help us," said Ehmet. "I told him he could go with us. Is that all right?"

"To my cousins'," Ali added.

"It's fine," Ehmet's mother said. "It's fine."

Ehmet had thought she would say that. She was pretty big on helping people. Especially kids. These days he had found he could help her.

"Mom, should we get our stuff? I don't think we should stay around here." He hoped she wouldn't ask him why. She didn't just then.

Ali tailed them when they started to walk toward the ruins. "You can just wait here a minute," said Ehmet.

Ali sat by the brook tossing in pebbles as the two walked to the ruins to retrieve what they had left there.

Ehmet clambered into the cart and gathered his things. He would have to rearrange his backpack to get everything inside. He took it off and unzipped it. His mother had climbed up onto the cart wheel. "Can you hand me my sweater?" Ehmet passed it to her. "And what were you doing . . . "

"Mom, shhh."

"I just want to know . . . "

"Shhh!" Ehmet insisted. But it was not just because he didn't want to answer the question. "I heard something," he whispered. They both listened.

Two voices could be heard coming from outside the ruins. Ehmet recognized one of the voices as Ali's. The other was a gruff man's voice.

"What are you doing . . . out of here . . . " Ehmet thought he heard the man saying, but it was difficult to be sure.

His mother climbed over the edge and into the cart, and huddled there with Ehmet. Her breathing was raspy and labored. Ehmet could not hear what else was being said. It occurred to him that if she coughed now, they could be found. His mother covered her mouth with a hand and breathed shallowly. The voices stopped.

They stayed huddled in the cart for a long time without hearing any noises. Then they heard someone climbing the spokes of the cart wheel.

Ali's head appeared. Ehmet was relieved, though not completely. It had occurred to Ehmet while they were hiding that he did not know Ali well, that Ali could have been talking to anyone, could have told someone they were here, or worse, led them over.

"He's gone," said Ali, as if he knew Ehmet's concern.

"Who was he?" Ehmet's mother asked.

"A Serb from our village, a Chetnik. He told me that I should leave. He knew my family had been taken away."

"What did you tell him?" Ehmet asked.

"That I was leaving. I ran into the forest so he would think I was going. I ran away from here so he wouldn't find you."

Ehmet was impressed.

"That's good, Ali. That he didn't come here."

"He did."

"He did?"

"I watched from the woods. He walked to the doorway and looked in. I hoped you were hiding."

"We were."

"So can we leave now?" asked Ali.

FOURTEEN

Mines

Ali knew his way over the mountains. They were taking footpaths he had traveled often. Ehmet was glad not to follow the roads, constantly on the lookout for vehicles, other travelers, or mines. Ali said he knew where the only mines were, far ahead, and he would avoid them.

Ali walked first. From time to time he would hop onto a boulder to scan the area with a pair of binoculars he had brought and which he otherwise left proudly dangling from his shoulder on their strap, bumping against him with each step. Ehmet's mother followed behind Ali. She had been having trouble walking, stumbling sometimes. She had to stop often to cough—wet, thick hacks, that rolled and shook her. Whenever she had a coughing fit, Ali would walk ahead to listen for anyone coming from the front and scan with his binoculars, and Ehmet would make sure no one was coming from behind on the trail. Then Ehmet would give her sips of mullein tea that he kept brewing by carrying the clear, herb-and-water–filled bottle tied on the outside of his backpack to warm in the sun. The tea soothed her, and the plantain leaves Ehmet crushed and would periodically apply to her feet provided some relief. After these breaks they would set off again.

Ehmet was used to his mother being well, capable, and active. That was the image he had of her, and it was hard to adjust to her being different.

At first, Ehmet didn't like being last in line as they hiked. He had become used to leading the way, to being the eyes and to making the decisions. But this was Ali's territory and Ehmet, if he led, would have had to turn to him anyway. So Ali led. After a while, Ehmet started to like being in the back. He could see Ali and his mother in front of him, and he had a chance to look around the forest in the daylight. When he and his mother had hiked at night everything had looked different, shadowy blocks and charcoal lines. Over time his eyes had become used to the night, and he could see more than he had thought possible in the darkness. But walking in the daylight, he could see details. The crackling lines of craggy old tree bark, and the flashing colors—reds, oranges, yellows, gold, and copper—of the oak and beech leaves reawakened and comforted him like a favorite song might. A series of long scratch marks high on one white-barked poplar tree reminded him that creatures perhaps even bigger than humans still made their homes here. He had an idea about who had left this sign.

Ali agreed. "Yup, bear."

"Bear?" said Ehmet's mother.

"They don't usually bother anyone," Ali added.

"Usually?" she questioned.

"Hardly ever."

Ehmet wanted to see a bear, though he did not want to surprise it. He had heard how bears could react if you suddenly came upon them or if they were with their cubs. Next to a berry bush, a curving footprint, bigger than any of the three of theirs and with claw points accenting the toe prints, was pressed into a muddy spot in the trail. Every time they passed another patch of berry bushes, Ehmet increased his vigilance. In the fall, bears foraged berries voraciously, preparing for a winter without food.

The three humans nibbled berries the animals had missed. Near one patch, they almost stepped in fresh scat with lots of berry seeds poking from it. That was as close as they would get to a bear just then.

They walked through the afternoon with Ehmet enjoying all that he could see.

"Stop!" Ali hoarsely whispered.

Ehmet walked right into his mother and Ali. He listened for other footsteps thudding, branches or leaves crackling under-foot, voices wobbling through the forest. He could not hear any-thing alarming. He peered ahead as far as he could see, to where the trail wound around the base of a cliff, scanned the surround-ing forest, and saw nothing unusual.

"What . . . " Ehmet began.

Ali pressed his lips together in a tight line, then barely opened them and muttered, "Mines."

"Where?"

"Right up there, on the trail," Ali said, pointing toward the base of the cliff.

"How do you know?" Ehmet asked.

"My father brought me here."

"Brought you here?" Ehmet's mother queried.

"Yes. He showed me where the mines are."

"How did he know?" Ehmet pressed.

"Because someone from our village lost a foot here. Blown off."

Ehmet had seen people other than his classmate, Mira, with missing limbs, mostly from rocket or shellfire, hobbling in the city streets. In Sarajevo there were not so many mines. But in the countryside, the plastic or metal packets that Ehmet thought resembled miniature, alien spacecraft, had been buried by the thousands and thousands. Millions.

Before school had been disrupted, when there were still classes, Mrs. Barisic had shown them a poster with pictures of different kinds of mines. It had been a strange science lesson from a teacher who had taught them so much about the living and growing—like rainforests and the brilliant frogs and crooning creatures that live there. Mrs. Barisic, instructing them about a science of killing and maiming. It occurred then to Ehmet that Mrs. Barisic would teach any science if she thought it might help them to know it.

He was glad that he knew something about mines so that he could try to avoid them on this journey. He had known that wouldn't be easy because mines were almost always buried under the soil or leaves. They lay out of sight, lurking explosively, ready to blast the unsuspecting. Ehmet had tried to be careful, but also not to think about them so that he could take each step without fear. He could not help but think about them now.

"We can go around," Ali said.

They left the trail and stayed close to each other as they made their way through the forest. Ehmet kept his eyes on the ground, alert for any signs in the soil or protruding shapes that might indicate a mine buried there. The damp carpet of leaves on the forest floor looked peacefully undisturbed except for the mushrooms that popped through in a funny array of shapes and colors—gnarly, orange trumpets; white-flecked red, rounded caps; and brown umbrellas as big as Ehmet's feet. Ehmet wanted to keep his feet and he tiptoed, stepping lightly and weaving, in hopes of dancing out of the way of mines.

Ehmet's mother was coughing again, but the dangers of the three of them being heard faded for the moment. She did not weave and pick her way along as carefully as Ehmet, her attention was focused on him. Every time Ehmet glanced up, he found her watching him move through the forest. She seemed unconcerned with her own well being, as she had ever since the night at his aunt and uncle's farmhouse. She had retreated since then to someplace deep within. Ehmet would love to hear her laugh again. He chuckled, thinking about her laughing in their living room back in Sarajevo, centuries ago. Both Ali and his mother stopped and looked at him, puzzled.

Ehmet's laughter seemed so out of place that he didn't know if he could explain it. "I was just thinking about us laughing in the apartment," he said to his mother. To his surprise, she smiled.

As they paused, Ali scanned the forest floor around them.

"He was up here picking mushrooms," Ali said.

"Who?" Ehmet asked.

"The guy from our village who got blown up. I mean his leg." Ali returned to searching the forest floor. "There are a lot of good mushrooms here. Some not so good."

Ali pointed at one of the red-capped, white-flecked mushrooms nearby. "This one is poisonous."

Ehmet knew that. It was one of the mushrooms he knew. It was called amanita. His grandparents had taught him about it when they walked in the forests near their farm, and he'd seen it pictured in fairytales and folk-story books. It was the kind of mushroom gnomes liked to sit on or witches would toss into a stew to poison an enemy. Ali picked a huge, plate-size, brown umbrella mushroom.

"You like mushrooms?" Ali asked.

Ehmet and his mother nodded yes. Ali picked another brown umbrella and put the two gently in his pack. Then he gathered up a few handfuls of the orange trumpets.

"Those are good," Ehmet's mother said. She really did like mushrooms. She'd bought them in the open-air market in the city before the war and even after it started. At the market stalls before the fighting there had been heaps of fruit, vegetables, cheeses, all kinds of food. Wild mushrooms grew, war or no war, and they were one of the few foods people were still able to gather in the countryside to eat or sell, though mines and snipers gave mushroom-gathering new dangers.

With the mushrooms stashed in his pack, Ali was ready to continue. As they passed the base of the cliff, he pointed at a stretch of the path visible through the trees.

"That's where it happened."

"I don't see anything," said Ehmet. "Didn't the explosion make a crater or something?"

"There was one," said Ali. "But whoever put the mines here must have covered the hole up again so people wouldn't know."

"Who do you think put them here?"

"I think Serbs . . . Chetniks. Some people in the village said it was Muslim fighters, to protect the village from Chetniks who might be coming. I think it was the Chetniks. Muslim fighters would have told us, don't you think?"

Ehmet was not sure what to think, who might have placed the mines, or why. And the mines themselves had no minds: they would not consider who placed them there, or who stepped on them, or why.

Once past the cliffs, the three continued winding down the trail on the other side of the mountains for another hour. It was getting dark, and Ehmet's mother's coughs were coming fiercely and often. She sat coughing on a rock by the trail.

"I thought you said it wasn't far to your cousins," Ehmet said to Ali.

"It's not. We can be there in a couple of hours."

"I can't . . . go . . . any farther . . . today," Ehmet's mother choked out between coughs.

Ehmet felt how worn down he was also. He had been walking in a dreamlike fog this afternoon. It struck him now that he hadn't slept since yesterday. The past day had stretched rubber band–like to hold more events than an ordinary week. He and his mother had walked all last night, Ehmet had gone into the village and back to the ruins, then the three of them had left hurriedly to cross the mountains. He had not slept at all for more than twenty-four hours. Clambering over the mountains rested and on a full stomach would have been difficult enough. He wondered how they had gotten this far.

The brushy forest around them did not offer any obvious shelter. But the rocky landscape was likely to offer a place. Ehmet helped his mother well off the trail to behind some bushes and a boulder where she would be out of sight to anyone using the path. She eased her head over to one shoulder, and within seconds of sitting dropped into sleep, her breathing raspy, yet not a cough. When she slept she had fewer coughing bouts.

Ali scrambled away, over and among the rocks to search for shelter. Ehmet searched the nearby mountainside, keeping his mother and her hiding place in sight below. He found a couple of overhanging rock ledges that would not offer much shelter in the coming night. At the base of a wrinkled face of rock, Ehmet spotted an opening, higher than he was tall. He ran over to it and looked in. A cave. The light at the opening quickly faded to blackness farther back. He could not tell how deep the cave was, but it was big enough for the three of them.

"Ali!"

◇

FIFTEEN

The Night

When they returned to Ehmet's mother, she was still sleeping. Ehmet talked to her to wake her up. She did not stir. This was a deeper sleep than he had seen. He hesitated to touch her, knowing how she had been since the night at the farmhouse. He touched her shoulder then jumped back, expecting her to react. She hardly moved, which startled him more.

"Mom?" Ehmet held her shoulder.

Her eyelids opened part way. "Mmm?"

"Come on."

With Ehmet tucked under one of her arms supporting her and Ali under the other, they made their way toward the cave. They chose their steps carefully to keep from stumbling and wound their way among the rocks, resting every few feet.

Dusk had turned to night, and it was almost as dark outside as it was inside the opening of the cave. Ehmet rummaged through his backpack and pulled out his flashlight and the broken one he had found in the car back in the village. He slid the batteries from the broken one into his own flashlight, flicked the switch, and smiled to himself as a beam lit the darkness. They were cave people, or would be.

The walls of the cave were relatively smooth, but a deep ripple formed a sheltered nook along the back wall. Ehmet took the blanket from his backpack, spread it out on the floor in the nook, and helped his mother to it. She collapsed and started to close her eyes.

"Mom, aren't you hungry?" Ehmet could feel his own stomach curling in on itself with hunger. The few berries along the way were long gone.

She shook her head weakly, "No."

"You should eat something." He reached for the only food that was immediately edible, the tin of sardines he had found that morning at Ali's. He popped it open with the key attached to the lid and offered her a sardine, speared on a fork.

"Not hungry," she mumbled.

"Then at least drink a little."

She took sips of the remaining tea Ehmet poured from the bottle directly into her mouth. After a few mouthfuls she turned her head, settled on the blanket, coughed a spell, and fell asleep.

Ehmet tucked the rest of the blanket over his mother and watched her face for a moment. The face that he had seen before turned upward in laughter, in a dance of expressions, now turned flat, quiet. His thoughts were interrupted by the hunger that leapt at him and moved him to reach for the can of sardines. The faint light of the flashlight glinted from the tin.

He cradled the open can near his nose. The smell was reminiscent of a beach where seaweed had been sitting a couple of days in the sun. To Ehmet the sardines were as luxurious as a heaping seafood banquet. He smelled them again, the sea and the food. Then he remembered Ali. Ehmet had been so many days with his mother only, he was unaccustomed to having anyone else at hand. He squinted around the cave. Ali was bent forward in a hump, his forehead touching the ground. He was praying. Ehmet realized then that a couple of times during the day when he had walked up on Ali, Ali had been standing up from a crouch and Ehmet thought he had been resting—Ali had been praying.

Devout Muslims prayed five times a day, bowing heads toward Mecca. Though Ehmet had visited a mosque on occasion, this prayer ritual was not the tradition of his family.

Ali raised his head and sat upright, signaling that he had finished his evening prayer.

"Hungry?" Ehmet asked.

"Sure am." They shared the tin, splitting the fifth and last sardine so that each would have two and half sardines, equal amounts. There was no food other than Ehmet's potatoes and the mushrooms Ali had picked that afternoon. Either would have to be cooked to be palatable. Ehmet had not built fires up until now to avoid attracting attention. Both Ehmet and Ali were too exhausted to cook anyway, so they went to sleep. Ehmet spread out his clothes to make a bed and pulled the jacket over himself for a cover. Ali curled up in clothes and a small blanket he pulled from his backpack. Ehmet fell asleep thinking that Ali knew how to take care of himself.

SIXTEEN

Where There's Smoke

Ehmet's mother awoke in the morning coughing and with a fever. By flashlight, Ehmet could see beads of sweat spotting her face. He reached to put his hand against her forehead like she had done so many times for him. He pulled his hand back as if from a burning pan, reacting to the shocking intensity of the fever. Her forehead was not warm to the touch. It was hot. Her cough was practically ceaseless, and rattled out in ragged, molten bursts. Liquid was boiling somewhere deep within, and Ehmet's mother was trying to hurl it out.

"Mom?"

She turned only slightly, looking at him hazily with half-lidded eyes. "Mmm?"

Even that murmured syllable was enough to kick her into another coughing fit. He tried to help her sit up. She lacked the strength just to hold herself upright. Her body oozed back to the ground in a rubbery mass.

Ali rolled over and rubbed his eyes. "What's up?"

"My mother's really sick."

"It's not far to my cousins'."

"She can't even sit up." Ehmet considered what to do.

He got the bottle of water from his pack and poured some onto a sock, the only one of that pair that had been in his pack, stuck in a bottom corner. It hadn't seemed useful to change just one sock, so it was his only clean clothing, and now his entire medical kit. "Doctor Ehmet." His mother had suggested once that he might become a doctor with his interests in science and people. He pictured himself a professional soccer player. A soccer-playing doctor. A doctor of feet. His thoughts spun as he eased the cool, damp cloth across his mother's forehead. He hoped he could help her.

She appeared to relax. The coughing continued, though in a less convulsive outburst. Her lips parted with a sticky clack. Ehmet noted a thick, yellowish coating glazing her lips. He raised her head slightly and poured a sip of water into her mouth. She swallowed and he gave her more until she turned her head down to rest again. He thought about what she would do for him. Soup.

"Ali, could you gather some sticks? For a fire . . . "

"I'll get dry wood." Ali disappeared into the brush outside the cave.

Ehmet unpacked the potatoes that he had gathered the first day by the old barn. There weren't many, though they'd added weight that he'd considered getting rid of. Now he was glad he had carried them. He cut them up with his pocketknife and put them with some water into the pot he had picked up yesterday.

Ali stood at the entry to the cave with an armload of sticks. "Here."

Ehmet and Ali heaped some of the sticks between two rocks outside so their fire wouldn't smoke up the cave. Ehmet made sure there were dry pine needles and a few pinecones in the base of the pile to get it burning well. He pulled the box of matches from the pocket of the jacket, where it had stayed since he had found the jacket at Ali's. He opened the box. It was half full of matches, each with a charred, burnt head. He examined them more closely, poking through them in disbelief. Ali's father, perhaps because he wanted to be sure that a discarded, still glowing matchstick would not ignite the countryside—had returned the used matchsticks to the box. No fire.

"Ali, do you have any matches?"

"No."

Ehmet pondered.

His eyes caught the binoculars Ali had dangling with him. "Can I see your binocs?"

"You can't see anything from here." The forest surrounded them. "You going to look for someone with matches?"

"You'll see." Ehmet held out his hand.

Ali gave him the binoculars. Ehmet started to unscrew one of the lenses. "Hey!" said Ali.

"I'll put them back together," said Ehmet. "I have an idea."

He held the loose lens toward the sun and studied the ground. A dot of light danced near the pile of fire-building materials. By moving the lens, Ehmet was able to focus a bright spot on the pine needles. He had done this many times with a magnifying glass when he was younger, burning holes in leaves. In a few moments the spot started to smoke. Ehmet bent close and blew on the embering pine needles. A tiny flame ate its way from the embers outward in a circle.

After a brief, smoky start, Ehmet was pleased to see the pile burning with clear flames in the cold, morning air. He had gotten used to living cold. Warming his hands over the fire felt good.

Ali sat warming himself by the fire and poking it with a stick, his reassembled binoculars again dangling in place on his chest. Ehmet brought the cook pot and set it over the fire, resting it on the rocks. "Can I use some of those mushrooms you picked?"

"Sure." Ali treated Ehmet with new confidence.

Ehmet added a few mushrooms to the simmering pot of potatoes, a bit of salt, and a good smelling leaf he had gathered for flavor. It was an unusual stew. Fortunately his mother liked mushrooms. Ehmet scooped some of the mix into a cup and took it in to her. She had hardly moved in her cave nest.

"Mushroom stew." She had not eaten or been interested in food since the day before yesterday. This was the only food they had, it was warm, and Ehmet hoped nourishing. "Come on, Mom." He helped her sit and held the cup to her lips.

With the slightest inhalation, she sipped some of the liquid from the cup. "Thanks," she whispered. Her cough rasped. She continued to sip and it quieted. "Mushrooms." She smiled wanly. It was good to see her smile, anyway. She finished about half of the elixir, then folded to the ground again.

Ali was still sitting by the fire warming. He and Ehmet finished off the stew. It wasn't bad. Forest gourmet, thought Ehmet. Flip, flip, a few fungi in the air, a couple of "zees powtatoes," and "voila, zee stowmack eez fool."

He and Ali wiped the pot as clean as they could with leaves and put out what was left of the fire by covering it with earth. Ali started stuffing all of his things into his backpack. Ehmet was repacking the pot, and the clothes he had used as a bed when shadows blocked the opening of the cave.

"We smelled smoke," intoned a gravelly voice.

SEVENTEEN

Better Not

All Ehmet could see were silhouettes in the cave entry. The sun had risen over the trees and bright light poured around three stark shadows, obliterating any details other than dark human forms with the spiny shapes of rifles protruding from them.

The one who had spoken first spoke again. "What are you kids doing here?"

"We're just going to my cousins'," Ali piped up.

"Alone? Just you kids?" The shadows swiveled searchingly, poking into the cave.

They could not see his mother from where they stood. She was hidden from their view in the nook where she lay sleeping. Ehmet debated about what to say. If they continued into the cave they would find her. Perhaps, just maybe, they would leave. He was about to tell them it was just he and Ali traveling when his mother coughed.

"Who's back there?" one of the invaders shouted. "Who's back there?"

All three of the shadowy men flattened themselves against the walls of the cave, with gun barrels pointing in the direction of Ehmet and his mother.

"It's my mother!"

"Put your hands up!"

Ehmet thought at first the demand was aimed at his mother, though since they still did not seem to have seen her, he realized it was probably directed at him. His hands were in his backpack, where they had been when the shadows entered the cave and interrupted his packing.

"Take them out! Slowly!"

He lifted his hands from the pack and opened them to show they were empty.

"Up, up!"

Ehmet held his hands up. Two of the three cave invaders held their rifles at Ehmet's head. The gravelly voiced man who had spoken first poked along the rock wall until he reached the nook where Ehmet's mother lay, now coughing profusely. He shoved the barrel of his rifle into the nook and flicked on a flashlight. The light glared in Ehmet's mother's eyes.

"No . . ." muttered Ehmet's mother.

"Don't hurt her," Ehmet growled.

"It is a woman," said gravel voice.

"My mother, I told you."

"Yeah, yeah." One of the two who had been holding his rifle on Ehmet moved away to peer at Ehmet's mother. "A woman, yeah." He spoke with an accent that Ehmet did not recognize. Seeing how he leered at her chilled Ehmet.

"She's sick," Gravel Voice said. He swung the flashlight beam around the rest of the cave. "No one else here, right kid?" Ehmet would have liked to tell him that hundreds of friends were waiting in the shadows. There was only Ali.

"Yeah, well . . ." said the leering one.

"Go tell the others," Gravel commanded.

Leering One shuffled out of the cave.

"What's your name?" Gravel questioned Ehmet.

It was not a question Ehmet wanted to answer. In this part of the world, it was most often names, not race or physical appearance, which defined what background people were from. There were names only a Croat was likely to have, other names Serbs used, likewise there were distinctive Muslim names. Ehmet sounded like, but was not a stereotypical, Muslim name. A few names were used across lines of background. He might have a little wiggle room. Ehmet told Gravel his name, and waited. From Gravel's stony expression he could not read a response.

"So where are you from?" Gravel asked. Where you were from could also make you an enemy these days. If your name did not define you clearly and you were from a place with many Serbs, you might be thought a Serb. Then Muslims or Croats could be an enemy. Being from a place that people thought of as Muslim might make him an enemy of someone Serb or Croat. Without knowing these men, he could not be sure who they thought their enemy was. Being from anywhere could be dangerous. Sarajevo was a place where Serbs, Croats, and Muslims had lived peacefully together for years. That in itself was enough to make some people angry, those who wanted to push separation. At least being from Sarajevo wouldn't immediately place him as part of one group or another. "Sa . . . " he started.

He was interrupted by Ali. "Rachman!"

Ali was shaking hands with one of several fighters who had returned with the leering man. The group was poorly armed and outfitted compared to most of the Serb and Croat fighters Ehmet had seen.

"He's from my village," Rachman said to Gravel, patting Ali on the back. "Muslim."

"And these?" Gravel motioned to Ehmet and his mother.

"Friends," Ali said. "Muslims from Sarajevo."

"Muslims from Sarajevo. Is a Muslim from Sarajevo even a Muslim?" laughed Leering One.

Ehmet hoped that this would not become a test of what kind of or how Muslim he was. He was certain Ali remembered that only his father was Muslim, and his mother Croat. Ali was trying to protect them by telling this group of Muslim fighters what they wanted to hear.

"I know the Quran," Ehmet added. He'd read it. He'd read several religious texts, including the Old and New Testaments, at the urging of his father who said he wanted Ehmet to know about the range of beliefs. Ehmet had found more similarities than differences in the various basic teachings and preachings, though he decided not to start that discussion with Gravel and his crew.

"So you are really going to your cousins'?" Rachman asked Ali. Rachman knew them. "It's true it's not a long walk from here."

"She's not walking anywhere," Gravel said of Ehmet's mother. Ehmet worried what he meant by "not walking anywhere" until Gravel continued. "She's real sick. If she is going, she will have to be carried."

Gravel and Rachman cut two, straight saplings from the forest and stretched a blanket between the poles. When they had finished building this litter, Ehmet helped his mother roll onto it. He jumped to one end of the poles. They started off with Rachman carrying the back and Ehmet the front. Leering One walked ahead with his rifle ready. Next was Ali. Gravel followed behind the litter, at the end of the entourage. The other fighters had disappeared into the forest. "We'll meet you tonight," Gravel had said to them as they left.

The makeshift litter was too heavy for Ehmet to lift for more than a few steps without stumbling. He set his mother down to readjust.

Gravel took off the rifle he had strapped over his shoulder while walking.

"Here," said Gravel, handing Ehmet the weapon. "Put it on. If I'm going to carry, you can have this thing bouncing against you." He picked up the poles Ehmet had been holding. Leering One had dropped back to the group, and was holding his gun on Ehmet.

"Strap it on your back," Leering One insisted, keeping his own weapon out and ready. "And you walk in front of me. I'll be watching you."

◇

EIGHTEEN

Family

Ali was right. It wasn't that far to his cousins' house. It took barely more than two hours to get there from the cave. The distance was easy for Ehmet after all of the walking he had been doing in the past days. At first he kept offering to carry his mother. Gravel insisted that he and Rachman would make quicker time. Rachman and Gravel complained little about the carrying, putting her down so they could rest every fifteen minutes or so. She was not a particularly large woman, and since she had not been eating in recent days was even lighter. Still, carrying her in the litter over the rough trail was not an easy task.

The challenge for Ehmet was to avoid sudden moves that might startle Leering One into shooting him. When a flock of crows burst suddenly from a treetop chasing a smaller bird, Leering One's immediate reaction was to swing his rifle up and fire in the tree's direction. The sound of the gunshots rattled all of the walkers.

"What are you doing?" barked Gravel.

"Achh. Could have been someone up there," Leering One said,

continuing to skittishly train his rifle barrel back and forth between the trees and Ehmet.

Ehmet was wary of Leering One as they walked.

The crows swooped overhead again, having been only briefly distracted from their pursuit of the smaller bird. Ehmet remembered an incident in the Giant, the tree he and Milan used to climb.

Long before the Giant had been cut, Ehmet and Milan were perched in the treetop when a chattering gang of crows dived at a nest trying to tear at eggs and young hatching birds. "Crows will even eat each other," Milan said. He had seen it happen. "Six crows ganged up on one, ripping into it."

They yelled at the big birds and waved wildly to scare them away, holding on to the tree trunk with one arm each, waving with the other. Usually that had worked to scare off crows. Not this time. The crows were unruffled. Ehmet decided to wave with both arms.

He fell from the branch he was sitting on and tumbled toward the ground. Ehmet had only a flying moment to wish for a parachute before he slapped across a branch. His stomach wrapped sharply around it and it rammed the air out of his body. He gasped and hung on to the branch, falling no more.

"You okay, Hot Pepper?" Milan had called.

"Uh," was all Ehmet could mutter. After a few moments, he was able to work his way along the branch and back up the tree to where Milan was being dive-bombed by an irritated crow. Ehmet waved again, though more slowly, somewhat painfully, with one arm. "Hey crows! We're alive. Not stuffed scarecrows! What, want to see me fly again?" After flapping around for a moment, the crows had resumed their perches and chatter. They didn't seem to take much notice unless something directly affected their own activities. Any fear they had appeared to be short-lived.

Ali's cousins were fearful seeing five people who they did not know arrive, the three fighters and Ehmet—the rifle still strapped to his back—and his mother, accompanying Ali. With the cousins' furtive, anxious looks at the rifle and him, Ehmet shifted uncomfortably. He was glad that Gravel immediately said to him, "I'll take that back now," unhooking the rifle and restrapping it to his own shoulder.

When Ali explained what had gone on and how he had been traveling with Ehmet and his mother since the village, his cousins were first upset, then they relaxed a bit. Since the fighters were Muslim and so was the family, Ali's cousins were not in obvious danger of being attacked. Yet the armed men could easily be part of one of the gangs of bandits who were plundering the land under the mask of war, so the family remained wary. The fighters had brought Ali safely to their home however, and in hospitality customarily extended to any guests, the family offered the travelers tea. All accepted without hesitation. Even Ehmet's mother took sips of tea gratefully between coughs, with fresh, sweet-smelling rolls that had been baked that day. It was both strange and comforting for Ehmet to be in a house that was a home; where people ate, slept, and conversed in an ordinary, and—what now seemed—remarkable way.

Conversation took an uncomfortable bend when Gravel asked if there was anyone in the family of fighting age. The mother responded that the family's children were all present and even younger than Ali, so were not good candidates. She quickly pulled out a recent family photograph to reassure that what she was saying was true. Rachman nodded in agreement. The father, Ahmed, walked with great difficulty—he had a noticeably twisted leg with the foot tipped outward at an unnatural angle, the result of a tractor tipping over on him while he was loading hay on a particularly steep hillside field, he explained. He could not traverse the countryside, with or without fighters.

Leering One turned to Ehmet. "You're old enough. And now you know how to carry a gun. You should be a fighter with us."

Ehmet was stunned. He answered only with silence.

"He needs to stay with his mother for now," said Gravel. "Until she's better."

"Ah then, for now. See you, Ehmet," said Leering One as the three fighters got up to leave. Hearing Leering One call him by name knotted Ehmet.

"Great rolls. Could we have the rest of these for our travels?" Leering One said. No one spoke. He did not wait long for an answer, he emptied the entire basket of rolls into the shoulder bag he had kept hanging at his side. "A bit of cheese to go with them would be wonderful, too. Thanks," and he added it. "And anything else you'll donate."

The house was quiet once the three left. Ali's cousins were practicing Muslims like Ali. They prayed after the fighters departed.

When they had finished their prayer and heard more of Ali's story, the mother, Aida, turned her full attention to Ehmet's mother, who was bundled on the sofa asleep. "She feels like she has a fever." She brought a thermometer and placed it in Ehmet's mother's mouth. "It's very high," Aida said. "How long has she had a fever?" she asked Ehmet.

"I think just since yesterday."

"We'll see what we can do. There's no doctor here in the village. The clinic closed after it was bombarded by the Serbs. Killed the doctor. They blew up the mosque, too." She disappeared into another room.

Ehmet pulled off his mother's muddy shoes, lifted her feet onto the sofa, adjusted a cushion under her head, and tucked the blanket around her. It was all he could think of to help her get comfortable.

Picking up his mother's shoes, Ehmet carried them outside the front doorway to scrape the mud off. He found a large, flat, wood chip to use as a scraper. The house was heated by a wood stove, and there was no shortage of chips in the yard from the chopping that prepared wood for the fire. Ehmet remembered the endless searches for wood to burn for heat in Sarajevo after the gas and oil lines to the city had been destroyed in wartime. Here at the edge of forest, the supply of wood appeared boundless.

Ehmet scraped absently until there was no more mud caked on the outside of the first shoe. As he put his hand into the second to hold it steady while scraping, he could feel mud that had seeped inside, and in the tip of the shoe he felt a lump.

He pulled his hand from the shoe and tapped the heel downward to knock the mud from the inside and dislodge the lump at the toe. To Ehmet's surprise, a small wad of bills tumbled out of the shoe. He pried the wad open, German marks and a few

American dollars. Not a fortune, but more money than Ehmet had seen in a long time. His mother had been hiding it, surely saving it for an emergency. She had had no opportunity to buy anything so far along the way. He looked around to see if anyone was watching him and the money. No one that he could see. He quickly stuffed the wad of bills into his pocket. It would be safer there for the moment than in the shoes, particularly if his mother wasn't wearing them. Ehmet checked the inside of the other shoe. It was not a bank. He carried the clean shoes into the house and set them back by the couch.

His mother was propped up with a few pillows, and Aida was giving her some liquid out of a teacup.

"Blackberry and elder tea, for the cough," Aida said to Ehmet.

She showed Ehmet a bottle of pills and poured one out. "Acetaminophen," she said, "to help lower the fever."

"Yes," Ehmet nodded. He recognized it. His mother had given him the same kind of pills when he had a fever.

His mother was able to swallow a few sips of the tea and the pill, then settled deep into the pillows. "Ehmet," she said in a raspy whisper. She raised her hand toward him. Aida put the teacup on a nearby table and slipped away from the sofa and into the other room. Ehmet grasped his mother's hand. With his other hand he reached over for the teacup and brought it to her mouth. "Great," she said to him after a few sips. He thought she meant the tea. "You've been doing great. You're grown. Almost grown anyway. Better than what you could get in a restaurant."

That was a family joke, "Better than what you could get in a restaurant." It was something that his grandmother had taken to saying about her own cooking in recent years. Ehmet's grandmother was a great cook. People devoured the tasty food she made and complimented her cooking. But of late, if people did not compliment her quickly enough, she would compliment herself. "This food is better than what you could get in a restaurant." The expression had come to be one of the highest compliments in Ehmet's family, used with a laugh for food and more. Ehmet's mother smiled at him, though her eyes were closed. It was the first time he had heard her try to joke since they had escaped his aunt and uncle's farm. Before that she had joked a lot. It was one of the essential ways she had dealt with things, whether they bothered her or not. She must be getting better.

Aida reappeared with another cup of tea that she handed to Ehmet. "It's good to have family. People who care what happens to you, anyway. A family of any shape or size. Your mother has been lucky to have you looking out for her." Ehmet took the tea and looked over at his mother. She had dropped into sleep again, her breathing an unsteady wet rattle. He was not sure how lucky she was.

Aida brought a damp cloth and wiped Ehmet's mother's face and head. His mother barely stirred. Aida picked up and wiped her hands as well. "Cool cloth. Should help lower her fever."

Ehmet had tried to do all he knew how. The cool cloth, even if a wet sock, had been right at any rate.

His mother rested better after being bathed with the cloth. Ehmet sat in a chair by the sofa watching her. Aida padded to the kitchen where Ahmed had been chopping something—Ehmet had heard a succession of thumps and thuds.

"Vegetables are chopped," Ahmed said to Aida. "I'm going out to cut some wood."

"We have plenty of wood. More chopping this afternoon?" Aida said.

"A choppy day," he answered. The kitchen door clacked shut.

Ehmet heard the rhythmic crack and clatter of chunks of wood being split one after another outside. Ali was chattering and laughing with his young cousins in the next room, a soothing murmur. Ehmet settled into the chair in warm, rapt luxury, with the smells of a meal being cooked wafting through the house.

When Ehmet awoke, the afternoon had passed. Outside it was dark. His mother lay on the sofa, the whistling sounds of her breathing still punctuated by bursts of coughing. Aida and Ahmed were bringing bowls of food from the kitchen to a long table where Ali and one of his cousins were setting silverware alongside plates.

Ehmet felt his mother's forehead. It did not feel hotter than before.

"I just took her temperature," said Aida. "It's gone down a little."

Ehmet gave his mother savory-smelling broth from a bowl that Aida brought. He gave her as many sips of broth as she would take—not many. His mother was so weak that opening her mouth took all of her energy; she could not lift her head from the pillows. She dozed again. Ehmet hoped that with nourishment and rest she would soon start to feel better.

He joined the family at the table. A real meal, with soup, steamed vegetables, and a rich noodle dish. "Enjoy," said Aida. Ehmet ate all he could. When he stood up from the table, his stomach was a stretched balloon.

Ali helped bring a thick quilt to the living room. Ahmed folded it to make a mattress for Ehmet next to the sofa.

Ehmet woke his mother to give her more of the broth. She took a few sips before dozing again.

"Good night," said Ehmet.

"Good night," Aida said as the family went off to the other rooms to bed. "Let me know if you need anything."

Ehmet stretched out, floating on his cloudlike mattress. He was full, comfortable, and warm for the first time in many days. If his mother were not sick, he thought, this would be heaven.

NINETEEN

The Rest

Ehmet slept for hours. He was awakened by an explosion, an eruption of his mother's heavy, wet coughing. Ehmet sat up. Her face was contorted, twisted as tree bark where a branch had broken off raggedly and was growing back over, gnarled, trying to heal itself. Ehmet could see glistening stars around her mouth, reflecting whatever light there was in the room. She let out another explosive blast of coughs.

Aida had heard her, too. She hurried into the room pulling a robe around herself, and switched on a lamp. In the brightness, Ehmet found that what he had seen reflecting around his mother's mouth were small puddles of saliva flecked with the red of blood.

"My God," said Aida. She groped for the thermometer case on the nearby table. Ehmet grabbed the cloth they had used earlier for cooling her, and wiped his mother's face clean.

Aida cradled Ehmet's mother's head with one hand while steadying the thermometer in the other. Her shaking coughs made it difficult to keep the thermometer in place or from possibly breaking. Ehmet slipped his arm behind her head and across her shoulders to try to hold her firmly through the wracking bursts.

When Aida checked the thermometer, Ehmet saw the cloud on her face. "It's gone back up. Even higher than before." She left the room. Ehmet could hear her leaving a phone message for a doctor in another village.

"I couldn't get hold of a doctor," she said to Ehmet when she returned with a clean damp cloth. "I'll try again soon."

Ehmet bathed his mother's face with the cool cloth. She seemed to relax again. Her cough subsided. But her breathing became a thin wheeze, air whispering in and out of her in whistling gusts. Ehmet held her hand. She turned her head and looked at him. He gently squeezed her hand. She smiled, then tipped her head back into the cushion.

Ehmet watched her resting.

TWENTY

Running on Empty

Ehmet's mother lifted her head from the pillow, gazed into the space in front of her, sat upright from the waist, and dropped back with eyes closed.

"Mom?" Ehmet took her hand, and when she did not respond put his hand to her face. Her face was drained of expression. He moved his hand near her nose and mouth. Where breaths, any wisps of air, should have been passing, there were none. He squeezed her hand. No response.

"Help!"

Aida stared at Ehmet's mother, and placed two fingers on her wrist.

"She's . . . gone," Aida said.

Ehmet couldn't believe it. He had thought of death as coming with a bang, rolls of thunder, crashings of doors or windows, loudness and chaos. He had seen it happen that way. Her death was quiet, yet more shocking. His own body was numb and empty. If someone tapped on his hollow shell the sounds would echo within like a drum. And all that he saw and heard was through a thick, hanging fog, as if he were far removed from everything and seeing only from a great distance.

People spoke to Ehmet—he guessed they might be speaking to him and he might be answering them, though the sounds he made were nothing more than grunts and abstract noises to him. Neither the questions nor his answers took on forms that he registered or remembered even a second later.

That day and a sleepless night passed.

"I think her cold turned into pneumonia. You couldn't control that," Ehmet heard Aida say from some distant place after the family awakened the next day.

"Maybe a doctor could have . . . " Ehmet murmured.

"We called the doctor. No one answered. Finally this morning I got hold of the family that lives next to the only clinic near here. The doctor has been gone for three days. He left the town in the last fighting. Or maybe they took him. Sometimes the fighters force the doctors to go with them, to take care of their own. Maybe he will be back. But there was no doctor, is no doctor . . . you did all you could."

Ehmet buried his head in his arms and silently wept.

"We should contact someone in your family," Ahmed suggested. In part at the mention of the word "family," Ehmet plunged into silence again.

"Who should we contact?" Ahmed asked gently when Ehmet surfaced.

Ehmet looked to Ahmed. "Can I try calling them?"

"Of course."

Ehmet tried all of the phone numbers he knew where it was even remotely possible he might reach his father. First he tried their apartment phone. It was out of order, as it usually had been since the fighting started, when one side or the other would destroy the lines. Same with the newspaper office phones.

Ehmet dialed his grandparents, and Aunt Boda and Uncle Petar's farm. No answer at either place. He dialed Milan's apartment. Maybe his best friend could help. Out of order. "I'll keep trying your family for you," said Ahmed. "And maybe we can get letters to them."

Ehmet wrote phone numbers and addresses where he hoped his grandparents and his father could be reached. He wrote the information for Aunt Boda and Uncle Petar's farm, too. He told Ahmed he didn't think they would be there. For the moment he didn't say why.

Though he kept trying, Ahmed could not reach anyone.

Ehmet tried to conjure the phone number of the house of a reporter friend who worked with his father. After several tries replacing digits that he was not certain of with different numbers, a phone rang. Someone answered. It was his father's friend, who haltingly told Ehmet that his father had gone to research a story on shelling of the Old City and had not been heard from in a week. People were looking for him. This friend and others from the newspaper had been searching. They would tell him about Ehmet and his mother when they found him, and give him Aida and Ahmed's phone number. The friend gave Ehmet his sympathies and wished him well, to which Ehmet could only mutter "Thanks."

Ehmet was tossed full force back into the void. From this empty place he watched Aida carefully washing his mother with damp cloths. She had moved her onto the table and draped a large, clean cloth over her body with her face still exposed. Aida had neatly combed her hair, and if it had not been for the waxy translucence of her pallid, white skin, Ehmet would have thought she looked good. He touched her cool forehead with two fingers.

Aida went to the kitchen for clean water and cloths. "She has bruises . . . " Aida said softly to Ahmed when she thought she was out of Ehmet's hearing range, "looks like she was attacked."

Ehmet stepped out into the yard. Ali had had the good sense to stop horsing around with his cousins since Ehmet's mother had died. They were waiting quietly outside now. Ali sidled to Ehmet and stood by him at the steps. "Hey," was all Ali said. It was an understanding "Hey," Ehmet thought. Ali knew what it was like to be on his own.

By that evening, they still hadn't heard from anyone in Ehmet's family.

"We'll have to do something," said Aida. Muslim tradition was to bury someone as soon as possible, preferably within a day.

• • •

The funeral preparations were as surreal and distant as his mother's death. Everyone was doing their best to be in touch with him, yet Ehmet was essentially far away, outside of his body and this place. Aida had dressed his mother cleanly and beautifully. It was his living mother, rather than this unreachable form, who kept approaching in Ehmet's thoughts

Ahmed had carefully built a coffin for her out of fresh pine boards. He was a skilled woodworker and had put special attention into what he was building, with respect for both Ehmet and his mother. By the time Ehmet had registered what he was building, the boards were taking the shape of what would be Ehmet's mother's resting place. Ehmet helped Ahmed sand the wood smooth until it shined. Ahmed showed Ehmet how to finish the surface to a bright sheen, through which showed the swirling grain that had grown with the wood in its lifetime. Dark round knots in the wood diverted the flow of the grain that continued around them.

The back-and-forth motions of the sanding were as repetitive as the thoughts Ehmet kept having, the whys and what-ifs. The motion of the sanding eventually became a meditation, which in its simplicity and lack of necessity for thought started to unlock him, freed him to be able to have a variety of thoughts and he began to awaken.

At the funeral service, he found himself looking around at the people who had gathered. He was peering as he had from his hollow in the tree when his mother first arrived from Aunt Boda and Uncle Petar's that night, with a mixture of anticipation and dread. That night hope had also been part of the mix. Now he would not see his mother. He felt like retreating back into the hollow.

Seeing the small group around him drew him out. He was amazed at the kindness of Ali, his cousins, and their family. Ehmet and his mother had been strangers to them, yet they had opened their home and done all they could to help. A few neighbors had gathered as well. People said prayers, and in a few words Ehmet tried to tell them what his mother had been like. He talked about her sense of humor, her strength before all this had happened and on their journey, about her love of people and of places. It was hard to tell people who didn't know her who his mother was, but he wanted to try. There was plenty of good to talk about. When he was finished saying what he could, the earth was heaped onto her coffin. For Ehmet, the thudding clods of earth hitting the lid of the coffin drummed the finality of her death. People drifted away, except for Ali and his cousins' family, who waited by the edge of the cemetery while Ehmet stood by her grave.

She was buried with her head facing Mecca, the Muslim way. "You know your family can move her later if someone wants to," Aida had said to him before the funeral. No one from his family had yet been in touch, and to Ehmet this seemed as suitable a spot as any.

He figured that if his mother could see this place she would like it. It was a small, country cemetery, at the crest of a hill with a scattering of ancient oak trees stretching bumpy roots into the meadow of high grass, light forest around it. Before all this, taking walks in the forest had been one of her great enjoyments. Ehmet could see her relax, any tightness or frowns leaving her face. There were several pictures of her sitting on hilltops alone, calmly looking over the countryside. She would have liked it here except for the gravestones, Ehmet thought. No, she'd probably have liked it anyway. She used to stop when they were traveling and wander through cemeteries, especially those that had been there for a long time, reading the stones. For her they were links to people—their stories, which she gathered from the names, the dates, the pictures, whatever was written and etched in the stones and in the place. Now she was one of those people, one of those stories, and Ehmet wondered who would pass and try to understand what her life had been.

The days at Ali's cousins' house passed for Ehmet in a broad, empty expanse marked by barely noticed bumps.

He continued to try to call his family. Ahmed continued to try the numbers as well, with no luck.

Ehmet again telephoned the house of his father's friend from the newspaper. No one had found his father yet. They would keep trying.

A week after his mother's funeral, Ehmet awoke anxiously. He felt out of place here, floating with no direction except to return again and again to his mother's death, or the present of an uneasy wait hoping that his father would be in touch. Aida and Ahmed had said that he was welcome to stay as long as he liked, they had made clear their welcome. Yet the group of fighters was still in the area. They had attacked Serbs and Croats in a nearby village, destroyed houses and a church, and in the past few days had pressed two boys close to Ehmet's age into joining them. They would likely return and insist that Ehmet join them, too. Leering One had already suggested as much.

Ehmet needed to leave, to do something.

He penned short letters to his relatives. Ahmed assured Ehmet that he would give the letters to people headed in the right directions and to the Red Cross, which had taken to delivering some mail after the postal service was put out of service. By afternoon, Ehmet was repacking his backpack. Ahmed, Aida, and Ali all tried to convince Ehmet to stay, but he swung the discussion his way when he reminded them that the fighters might return for him. They could not argue that that was not a possibility. Still, they tried to convince him that he could stay in the area, that it would be safer than traveling. Ehmet was not to be convinced. He had already come this far trying to get to his grandparents and he thought he could handle whatever lay ahead.

Ahmed went over Ehmet's map, what he thought would be the best route to Ehmet's grandparent's house. Aida packed as much food as Ehmet could carry, and Ali gave him a compass.

"You're pretty good at getting around. Now you can really check out north and south," Ali said.

"Keep in touch," Ahmed said, handing Ehmet a piece of paper with their phone number and address on it. The address was easy to remember, not much more than the village name. "We'll let your father know where you went. And contact us if you need anything. Anything."

Ehmet tried to give Ahmed and Aida some of the money he had found in his mother's shoe. They refused.

"Please keep it for your journey," said Aida.

◇

TWENTY-ONE

The Border

Traveling was physically easier than before. Ehmet had rested in the comforts of Ali's family's home, he now had food and clean, warm clothes. His legs were stronger from all the walking, then resting, he had done. Walking itself seemed effortless, he didn't notice it anyway. Often he would break into a run. Running released him from the ragged pace of his thoughts. He ran in long bursts, farther than he had ever run before, his mother's death igniting him ferociously.

He would run for a while, then walk, then run again. Ehmet followed the route that he and Ahmed had laid out on the map. The compass Ali had given him helped when he was uncertain about which direction he was heading, though now he had the sun to help orient him as well.

He had decided to walk during the days for a number of reasons. He had rediscovered at Ali's cousins' house that he slept better at night than he had during the days before he got there. Whether it was his natural internal timekeeping or the unsettling possibility of someone stumbling onto him, his daytime sleep had not been that sound. Sleeping nights, he awoke better rested, so he had plenty of energy to walk and jog at a rapid pace. Details of the landscape were much more visible in the daylight, which helped in being able to quickly find his way and his foot-ing, too. Besides, walking alone at night was a much darker prospect than it had been with his mother. Fear of daytime encounters was trounced by pain.

In the evenings, Ehmet found places other than the kinds of abandoned buildings he had looked for to shelter his mother. He found haystacks at the far edges of fields or dense umbrellas of low-hanging, evergreen boughs in the forests, became expert at pulling fallen branches together to make hard-to-see shelters into which he could tuck himself away for the night.

In the daylight it was easy to see the roadways he was follow-ing. Ehmet could be easily seen as well. He felt reckless. What did it matter? It was mostly his desire to stay out of touch with peo-ple, not to have to talk or interact, that kept him out of sight—cutting through forests, the overgrown edges of fields, along stone walls. When he heard vehicles coming he ducked and hid until they passed. He watched for people, and the few he saw by roadblocks, in the fields, or close to buildings were carefully avoided. He took time to skirt around towns and villages. Still, he figured he was covering ground at least twice as fast as he had been while walking nights. At this rate, he should be able to reach his grandparents in another week or so.

Several days after he had left Ali's cousins', his food supply was noticeably lower. Aida had been generous, but Ehmet could only carry so much in his backpack, and he had been eating substan-tially. His appetite had returned at Aida and Ahmed's and his stomach had expanded to accept all that they had offered. He had eaten like the growing being he was, who needed fuel to turn into muscle and bone and brain cells. Well, maybe no more brain cells—Mrs. Barisic had told the class that scientists had sup-posed we were each born with a limited number of those cells. After that, Ehmet remembered reading a news article his father had written about some recent studies that showed maybe you could add brain cells under the right circumstances. There's always hope, Ehmet thought. Now he was thinking of food, and wondering how he could supplement what he had in his pack. He searched for berries in the bushes along the way. It was too late in the fall—only a few shriveled or moldy ones still hung unappetizingly from the branches.

Money, now he had money. He hadn't spent any of it and had nearly forgotten about using it, it had been so long since he'd had any. By avoiding towns and villages he also had no access to the shops in them. To enter a shop meant the probability of coming into contact with a number of people. He decided to keep his eyes open for a friendly looking farmer or individual he could buy food from. Not wanting to show the wad of money if he did encounter someone, he pulled off a few bills, deciding on a mix of some American dollars and some German marks. The monies issued by the old Yugoslavia and the new Bosnian and Serb governments trying to form countries were almost worthless. Their tiny values fell closer to zero with each day of chaos. Ehmet put some of the dollars and marks into his pocket at the ready and hid the rest.

A river appeared before a likely looking person did. For Ehmet it was a river of food. He fished out the piece of line he'd squirreled away and the hooks Ali had given him and turned over flat, rounded, river stones until he found a water insect to use for bait.

The fish were cooperative, or one was. He cleaned it with his pocketknife and found a stomach full of insects the fish had eaten. The problem was, how to eat it? Ehmet had heard of sushi, the Japanese raw-fish food. That was not a meal he was anxious to try at the moment. He cooked up another plan.

There was a good breeze gusting over the water. On the stone beach that lined the shallow river edge, Ehmet found two large rocks and placed them so that there was a small canyon between, oriented so the breeze would sweep through. He speared the fish on a stick that he rested on the two rocks, stretched over the space between them.

He carried his backpack up a good distance away from the river and stashed it in the bushes. With dry twigs and grasses he gathered on the way back down to the river, he built a pyre between the rocks—grasses heaped at the bottom, then piling on bigger and bigger twigs, under the fish. He snapped a match. The wind blew it out. He snapped a second to his tinder construction. Fanned by the breeze funneled into it, the flickering kindling burst to flame with almost no smoke. As soon as he saw the steady flame, Ehmet raced back to where he had secreted his backpack and hid himself in the brush.

From his hiding place he could watch the cooking and keep a lookout in case someone smelled or spotted the fire. Ehmet thought that unlikely as the breeze over the river was dispersing the smoke and smell, making it difficult to track down from any distance.

When drops from the cooking fish spattered on the fire and released momentary coin spots of smoke, Ehmet guessed the fish was close to being done. Putting his backpack on, he scanned the surrounding area, and seeing no one, raced down to his fire pit. He grabbed one end of the stick, pulled it and the fish from the fire, kicked sand and small stones over the blaze to put it out, and hurried away. Careful to keep the fish from falling, he hopped up the riverbank. Well away from the river and fire pit, Ehmet stopped running and tucked himself behind a boulder. The fish was still warm and smoky, and made a good dinner, for which he was grateful.

He continued in the direction he'd been headed before his fishing expedition, walking through increasingly steep and mountainous terrain. From the map and the landmarks he saw around him, it appeared that he was nearing the border between Bosnia and Croatia. There was certain to be a roadblock or border post with guards where the road crossed the border. Ehmet had avoided other roadblocks, where armed men guarded gates or parked vehicles and questioned anyone who tried to pass. This would be different. He had to cross a border, a place where two newly declared countries were trying to draw a line between themselves. Ehmet wondered what he would encounter.

Approaching the invisible line, he left the roadway and climbed higher and higher up a mountainside so that finally he could see a border-crossing post far below—a gate across the road and a small building with soldier ants attending it. He clambered over rocks and dodged trees. At one point he saw a trail, but stayed off of it. It looked too well used, wide, and worn. There were fresh footprints in the mud. Ehmet did not want to encounter anyone, or groups of anyone—gangs, smugglers, fighters—who might be lurking around the border.

In the distance he heard dull thuds that he knew to be mortars, cannons—a mix of the two—and pops of rifle fire coming from a mountain ridge a few miles north. Across the valley to the east, he could see plumes of smoke and flickering, orange shreds of flames rising from buildings in a town. From this distance, he could not see people in the town, yet knew they must be there. He had been where they were. He could picture them sitting in their living rooms before fighting started, then perhaps diving under beds or into basements when they realized the possibilities. Ehmet would have liked to think that whoever was firing at the town from the mountainside saw no people there, did not know what they were doing to people in the town. But he knew that in the hills around Sarajevo the shooters used binoculars and telescopic sights so they could see the people they were shooting at. How could you fire at someone walking to the market to try and buy milk? That took a kind of blindness, anger, or hatred that Ehmet could not grasp. Ehmet was angry, particularly when his thoughts drifted to those who might have attacked his mother. Yet it was not a blind anger that would enable him to strike at just anyone available.

Ehmet felt the cold. He dug into the backpack for his sweatshirt and encountered his mother's sweater. It was the only thing of hers he'd brought with him. Aida had suggested it. "You should have something of your mother's," she'd said. Since his mother had no belongings with her besides what she had on, there'd been little choice. He had picked out the sweater and Aida washed it. It smelled fresh from drying on a line in the country air. Ehmet had seen his mother in this sweater so many times . . . He'd been brushing back such thoughts the past few days.

Whoom. A thunderous roar from above rocked Ehmet. Instinctively he ducked. When he looked up, he saw the silver underbelly of a jet plane bolting along the mountain ridge.

Before he had time to register what was happening, there was an explosion—a fireball and dark blob of smoke, up the ridge. The plane had dropped a bomb on the area from which the mortars and cannons had been fired. With Serbs, Croats, Muslims—so many groups fighting—at times it was hard to know who was firing at whom. Ehmet wondered whose plane it was; he had not seen the identifying markings. Many people—primarily Muslims or Croats—had been hoping for other countries, perhaps the European and North American NATO members, to send planes to help against attacks such as the firing from the ridge that Ehmet had just seen. They had waited and waited. Maybe it was a NATO plane. It was likely someone else's. The Serbs had the warplanes that had been Yugoslavia's air force before the breakup, and the Croats had a few. Bosnia had none.

The jet was gone as quickly as it had come. It shrieked away in an instant. Black smoke from the bomb's explosion continued to leak in a plume from the mountainside. For a while there was quiet, no gunfire, then scattered mortar and rifle fire popped from the ridge again. There was no cannon fire, so possibly the cannon had been knocked out in the bombing, but the attack continued.

Ehmet was anxious to move on.

He pulled his backpack straps into position and straightened to stand. The mountainside was steep, and Ehmet wanted to ascend it as quickly as possible. He wrapped his hands around small tree trunks to help pull himself up, hopped over boulders and around bluffs.

Reaching the mountaintop, he pulled out the map to orient himself. A dotted line on the map stretched along the ridge. Somewhere nearby was the border. He could be sitting on it, there was no line etched on the mountain. Ehmet looked back over the slope he had just climbed, land that people called Bosnia, and at the slope ahead on the other side that he would be descending, that was called Croatia. Each was tree-and-rock covered, practically mirror images of each other. The two countries were indistinguishable at this point except for plumes of smoke and gunfire that currently pocked the Bosnian side.

As Ehmet made his way down the slope into what he assumed to be Croatia, he breathed better, both from the ease of descending and the relief of being in a part of the countryside that as far as he could see was not war torn. The sounds of gunfire were becoming more distant.

Evening took hold. Ehmet tucked himself into a hollow under the low-hanging boughs of an evergreen tree, and to the rhythm of the now-faint booming, fell asleep.

The next day he continued into Croatia. Ehmet caught sight of a roadway snaking below, and headed toward it so that he could use it as a guide again, staying out of sight as he had done before. He had no idea who he might meet if he were on the road. Whether visible or not, this was still near a border, in fact, a highly disputed one. At the very least, he was a Bosnian crossing into Croatia, and some Croats were as ready to attack Muslims as were some Serbs. In areas of Bosnia where Serbs had not killed or driven off Muslims, some Croat militias had been willing to do the same. With one parent of Croat background, the other Muslim, Ehmet had never wanted or had to decide between the two. Left side Muslim, right side Croat? Like almost half the kids he knew, who came from mixed backgrounds, too, he considered himself Bosnian, because Bosnia was now the country where he lived. Before that, Bosnia, Croatia, and Serbia had all been part of the country called Yugoslavia. In the past year or so, some people from each region had tried to separate parts of Yugoslavia and the population into distinct countries—Croatia, Bosnia, Serbia. They fought to create new borders, and to move people. Borders suddenly appeared—a strange phenomena to Ehmet— being drawn and redrawn around places or even a person. He could fall on one side or another in someone else's judgment since a border was where anyone put it, with hatred or affection in the heart of the line drawer.

The forest he was passing through was a mix of old, large trees: oak, beech, and pine. On the shaded, leaf-covered floor not many bushes grew to block his progress. He hiked readily, keeping the road in partial view until he found himself at the bank of a river. Waters of the river foamed in white rapids and curled around boulders, below which were deep-looking, dark pools. He would have to cross the river one way or the other to continue. It was fast flowing and noisy, with the *tunk-tunk* of stones bouncing in the current, too treacherous to wade. The most obvious way to cross would be the bridge that carried the nearby road.

Ehmet turned and started toward it. Around the first bend in the riverbank he stopped, startled. He had almost run into someone fishing.

◇

TWENTY-TWO

Flying

The fisherman was an old man. Ehmet saw that as soon as he got over the surprise of stumbling upon him. White hair stuck out from under his canvas cap. He was in mid cast, the long line arcing from his fishing rod in a huge, graceful S. The artificial fly at the end of the line landed gently on the water's surface at the edge of a pool, next to a boulder. A circle of ripples emanated from the spot where the fly landed. The fisherman stripped out an arm's length of line so that there was enough slack to let the fly float across the pool with the current, then started pulling the line back in with his left hand, letting it coil in a neat pile by his feet.

"Do you fish?" the old man asked in Croatian. Ehmet had not seen him take his eyes off the water, yet he had obviously seen Ehmet.

"Yes, a little." He answered the old man in his best Croatian accent. Luckily he'd had plenty of chances to practice it with his grandparents. Ehmet had fished for years with spinners or bait. He had only started fly fishing a couple of years ago.

"Then you know what it's like to try to pretend you are an insect."

Ehmet hadn't thought of it that way before, it was a good description of what you had to do, pretend you are an insect, or at least know enough about insects to make a fake fly, fabricated of hairs and feathers, look as if it were a live one.

"I like to think I have a reasonable-sized brain," said the old man, chuckling. "But it's amazing how difficult it is to be an insect that has practically no brain at all."

The old man cast the line again. He waved his right arm deliberately and smoothly, as a dancer might. Line kept streaming out of the rod until there was enough to reach well across the river. The fly hung, just a speck in the moist air above the water. Close to the far bank, the fly bounced off the side of a rock into a pool. The old man jiggled the rod slightly and the fly moved in response. "Like an insect that fell off the rock." The fly sputtered on the surface, then was sucked under the water and out of sight. Immediately the old man raised the tip of the rod slightly while pulling the line in, keeping it taut. The rod bent toward the water in a quivering arc—the old man had caught a fish. He pulled it in slowly and firmly, never letting the line go slack as the fish darted from one spot to another. It leapt into the air headfirst and slapped its tail on the surface of the water, hopping across the river. It was a big trout, golden and speckled. The old man kept it on the line and pulled it close to him. Rather than pulling the fish out, he reached underneath it in the water and with an adept, almost imperceptible, twist released the fly from the trout's mouth. He kept his hand resting under the trout's belly for a moment. "All right then, off you go." With two strong sweeps of its tail, the fish dived freely toward its watery home.

Ehmet watched the old man make several more casts before catching another fish. This one was not as big. The old man kept it and put it in a basket on the bank. Another fish was already in the basket. "That's enough," the old man said.

Bright tangerine reflections of light spattered the river between long, spidery, tree shadows. The afternoon was closing.

In his hurry to get farther into Croatia, Ehmet had not eaten since midday, when he had crunched the few crackers that remained from Aida's supplies.

Ehmet did not want to linger here long enough to go fishing himself. There were two fish in the basket, and only one old man. "Could I buy one of those fish?"

"Buy?"

"I'd be happy to pay you." Ehmet reached into his pocket to withdraw the bills he had peeled earlier from his money stash.

"And I would be happy to have you join us for dinner. No paying."

"Us?"

"My wife and I. Unless you have other plans, that is."

"Uh." Ehmet hesitated.

"Just two old geezers, we'll do you no harm."

Ehmet sized up the old man. He had said nothing to indicate malice. He seemed kind, and if he wasn't, Ehmet was certain he could overpower him physically if need be. As soon as they got to the old man's house he should be able to see if just he and his wife lived there.

"All right, thanks."

"I was hoping you would say that."

The two of them climbed the bank next to the bridge. The old man was wiry, thin, and nimble. He stepped lightly up the bank, and bounded like a deer over the top. Ehmet listened for the sounds of vehicles before stepping onto the roadway and across the bridge. He hurried, the old man trailing behind him. Reaching the far end of the bridge, Ehmet took a few steps off the road into the forest. Habitually now, he stayed off roadways. It occurred to him that he did not know what route they were going. Ehmet was so used to finding his own way, he had automatically leaped to the front. He looked over his shoulder.

"That's fine," the old man said. "Getting off the road. A good idea. I usually do myself these days. No fighting here now, but there was not long ago. Lots of patrols and who knows what else pass."

They kept to the forest.

Through the trees they glimpsed a truck with uniformed soldiers on the road below, racing toward the border. Ehmet dropped to the ground. "Croat patrol," said the old man. "They're already gone." Ehmet got up and brushed himself off somewhat sheepishly. The old man hadn't missed a step.

"You've been walking far?" the old man asked.

"Pretty far. I'm . . . from a ways away."

"I knew you weren't from around here. I know most everyone in this area. Lived here a long time. Besides, not many people out for a walk would carry a blanket and all that gear you've got."

Ehmet reached over his shoulder and felt his backpack. Part of the blanket and a pot handle were sticking out from under the top flap.

"We turn here," the old man said. They had arrived at a junction where a single lane, unpaved side road joined the paved main road they had been following. "I think we can walk on this road. There are only a few farms besides ours. Hardly ever any traffic."

Ehmet walked silently with the old man on the country road. The sun had set, and the flamingo, rose, and red streaking of the sky had given way to dark, punctuated by the moon and first stars. The old man appeared sure enough of his footing. Ehmet wondered how many times he had walked here at night.

"This is it." The old man led Ehmet up an earthen driveway toward a farmhouse with a barn behind it. Ehmet had a new affinity for barns, having slept in their soft hay so many times. "What is your name, by the way? I should find out before bringing you home to Danica. My name's Jakob."

A distinctive name, Jakob, Ehmet thought. "Ehmet," he responded.

Jakob opened the heavy, wooden, farmhouse door. In the room, seated reading in a comfortable looking overstuffed chair, was a woman who appeared to be similar in age to Jakob. She peered up from her book as they entered, long wavy strands of red hair streaked with gray falling from a loose bunch at the back of her head. Her hair contrasted with the plush, green velvet of the chair. Ehmet imagined a fire glowing in a meadow. He felt strangely welcome.

"So who is this?" she asked Jakob.

TWENTY-THREE

Jakob and Danica

After introductions, they began preparing dinner. Danica peeled and cut several large potatoes and chopped some curly-leafed green kale. "From our garden," she said. "Kale is sweeter after the frost."

Jakob cleaned one of the fish and Ehmet helped by cleaning the other.

Ehmet looked at his. "Why did you keep this fish when you let the bigger one you caught before it go?"

"I let a lot of fish go. In fact, most of those I catch, I let go. But these two fish were hooked badly. They would not have lived. I only keep what we can eat. The rest I release. Some of the fish in that river I've caught—or they've caught me—many times."

"He makes a good insect," Danica teased.

"Or a good Croat," Jakob retorted. They both laughed, though Ehmet could not find what was funny. Jakob saw Ehmet's blank expression. "I've learned I am many things. I'll explain to you later."

Danica sautéed some onions with the kale and boiled the potatoes. Jakob placed sprigs of fresh herbs on the fish and put them in the oven. Soon the kitchen was filled with rich smells. Jakob spooned whole cucumber pickles out of a ceramic crock.

"His pickles," said Danica. "He makes the best pickles."

"Everybody has their specialties," Jakob said.

Before dinner, Danica brought out two candlesticks, lit two candles, and cupped her hands around them while Jakob chanted words in a language Ehmet could not understand.

"Hebrew," said Jakob. "Friday night. For me, a Jew, the beginning of the Sabbath."

Another light went on in Ehmet's mind. His father had sometimes lit candles on Friday nights, said he had seen his great grandmother, a Jewish woman who had married a Muslim, doing that every Friday night and liked the custom. Except for that great-grandmother, his father's family had been Muslim as far as Ehmet knew. She had died long before Ehmet was born, and he did not know much about what it was to be Jewish.

The dinner was as good in taste as it had smelled while cooking. After the meal, Ehmet sat back in his chair and placed his hands across his full belly.

"Good?" Danica asked him.

"Really good. Thank you."

"So," said Jakob. "I told you I would explain some things. You like stories?"

"He can talk," said Danica, pointing at Jakob.

"That's all right," said Ehmet. "I like stories." He liked the idea of just listening for a while, and he was full and comfortable. He settled in for the ride.

"It starts with her," Jakob said.

"So you blame it all on me?" Danica teased. She was pleased, not upset.

"Not blame. Just where it starts. We met at the university in Zagreb. That was a few more than a few years ago. You know, just before the Second World War. I liked her the minute I saw her."

"And I liked him about a minute and a half later."

"It doesn't necessarily happen that way. You know that, right? Sometimes love develops slowly. Always does, I think. As you get to know the person, know many sides, visible and hidden, and you go through things together. At first I saw something of her beauties, her red hair, she looked pretty good from the outside, and when she spoke she seemed kind, intelligent, open minded, and gutsy."

"Gutsy?" said Danica.

"Chutzpah, yes. You know you've got it."

"Yes, okay. I've been with you a long time. I'll go along with that."

"And along with the story?"

"If I agree."

"Okay, so we're continuing. The war starts, the second one, with the Nazis, we're hearing about the Nazis, but at first it's hard to believe what we hear. A few people left the country when they heard. Most stayed though. Then there were the Ustashe, Croats who decided to be Nazis. How could the place we had been a part of since birth, some people we thought we knew, turn sour, turn against us? Even more difficult to accept. People have much better possibilities."

Ehmet thought of Darko, Ali, and other people he knew who held hate and blame of one group or another close at hand. Jakob stood up from the table and retrieved a photograph from the top of a cabinet.

"This is . . . was my family," said Jakob, holding the faded black-and-white photograph close so Ehmet could see it. "That's me." He pointed to a boy in a slightly rumpled suit. Ehmet could imagine him playing around just before the picture. "And that's my brother, he escaped and lives in Los Angeles. That's my sister, she escaped and moved to Israel, later, when it was made a country. She still lives there. The rest of the people, my parents, grandparents, aunts, uncles, cousins—twenty-three people—all killed, mostly in the camps. A picture with twenty-six people, and three left." He turned the photograph over. On the back were people's names. Below twenty-three of them were penciled Xs.

"I'm sorry . . . ," said Ehmet. It was all he could think of to say.

"I appreciate that," said Jakob. "But that is not why I am telling you this story. There are some things I want you to know, and about the good in people, too. A lot of foolishness going on these days."

"These days?" said Danica.

"Okay, foolishness is possible anytime. I've been a fool myself at times."

"Not that kind of fool. If you are a fool, you are the fool I love."

"So, I can continue?"

"Being a fool?"

"Since you said you loved one, I'll go on. I'm Jewish," said Jakob. "Though I consider that a private matter. The Nazis and the Ustashe didn't. Somehow it was their business. Twenty-three people, members of my family, were killed with the excuse they were Jewish. That is the foolishness I refuse to accept. One is Jewish, one is Serb, one is Croat, one is Bosnian, one is Christian, one is Muslim, one is Gypsy, one is maybe from the moon, to try to make the other guy the bad guy. Serbs, Gypsies—you know the Gypsies call themselves Romany—the Ustashe killed them also. But I said I wanted to tell about good, too."

"I would appreciate that," said Danica.

"You should, you're part of it. We left the university in Zagreb together, and she brought me here, to the countryside, to her family, all Croats. In this region few people were Ustashe. In fact, some worked against the Ustashe. I joined them. And her family hid me. Well, I didn't really hide, I was part of the community. I worked the farm, even went to town once in a while with the family so people wouldn't get suspicious of this mystery man living on their farm. It was dangerous for them, if anyone had found out. Danica and her family, a couple of them, knew about me being Jewish, told anyone who asked that I was Croat, which I am, too. Born and lived here. It was ironic, a Croat having to masquerade as a Croat. So I was treated as a human being, just as any human being should be treated, I think, as part of things. Does this make sense to you?"

"Yes," said Ehmet.

"Part of the reason I tell you all this . . . you're Bosnian. During the war I had to use a Croat name. 'Jakob' was right away Jewish. Even if you don't tell them your Muslim-sounding name, your accent can give you away. You could be Croat, Muslim, or Serb—doesn't matter much to me. But it will to some people. Who you are is your business, not everyone else's. I just want you to be careful. It appears you have been so far, to get here on your own."

At that, Ehmet could not hold back any longer. Danica and Jakob had been understanding enough not to press him about who he was and where he'd been. They still weren't probing: He wanted to tell them. In a flood of bits and pieces, he told them of leaving Sarajevo, about the incident at the farm and his and his mother's flight, about her dying, about not knowing where his father was, and now being on the way to his grandparents.

Danica stood and wrapped an arm around him.

"The things that have happened . . . You have been swimming upstream," said Jakob. "You are stronger than you may know."

For some time they sat in silence. Ehmet collected himself, his breathing changed from stuttered inhale to deep exhalations.

"Why did you stay here?" Ehmet asked Jakob, "When there were people around who hated you, might have killed you, just because you were Jewish?"

"That was a very personal decision. I knew of course because of Danica, because of her family, because of friends, that all Croats were not hateful toward Jews. It was a bad time, many people were confused. During the war it was dangerous. Fortunately, it worked out for me as people around here thought of me as Croat. In some ways it was an act of defiance to stay after the war. I told them I was Jewish, I wanted them to know. By that time they knew me as a person and they had accepted me. Most did, anyway. A few could not reconcile my being a Jew with being 'one of them,' and said 'no, you're not Jewish, couldn't be.' Then it was theirs to sort out the difference between some image and a person."

"I suggested he should try to escape many times during the war," said Danica.

"There's no escaping you," said Jakob. "Besides, I felt relatively safe with you and your family. I was lucky."

"You were," said Danica. "You know I would have gone with you. I offered."

"I know. But we never went. It wasn't so easy, escaping, either. Many people died trying. My brother and sister spent years in refugee camps trying to make their ways to new homes. And I've been in Los Angeles, and in Israel. Each place has its own peace to make."

"So you'll stay here?" Ehmet asked.

"As long as I can still fish. Maybe when I am too old, I'll look for a palm tree in one of those deserts," Jakob laughed.

"I? What happened to we?" Danica asked.

"We, of course. You like fishing, too."

"And palm trees. Though I prefer the smells of our pines. We have our differences," Danica said to Ehmet. "We work things out. That's a relationship. Loving someone, knowing that they don't have to be just like you, behave just like you. It's easier said than done, but we've both been willing. More than willing. You have someone?"

The question caught Ehmet off guard. He'd often thought of Mira as he walked, realized how much he admired her, enjoyed being with her the few times they'd been able to be together in Sarajevo, at school, at the dance. There hadn't been much opportunity to know how it would be beyond that. "Ah," he answered.

"So you do. You'll see, then."

TWENTY-FOUR

◇

Wake Me Up Oily

Jakob and Danica awoke early, so Ehmet did as well. Not as early as they did though—he woke up to smells of breakfast. Jakob was cooking eggs. "He makes a wonderful omelet," said Danica.

"And you make salads and invent dishes with vegetables from our garden like nobody else."

"The kale last night was great. I didn't even know I could like kale," said Ehmet.

"Okay you two, I am retiring, quitting while I am ahead," Danica said.

"I thought you had retired, I'm cooking breakfast," said Jakob.

"So that is your full-time job?" Danica asked.

"Maybe it will be for today."

Ehmet did not think that was likely. They were both active people. He hoped he would be as energetic when he was eighty. Being in their home was like being with his grandparents, though they were younger than Jakob and Danica. Ehmet appreciated being in the midst of this good humor, banter, and food, yet looked forward to arriving at his grandparents'.

"I hope we didn't wake you up too early," said Danica.

"It's all right," said Ehmet.

"You know, a lot of people as they get older wake up earlier and earlier," Jakob said. "We don't sleep so much."

"Yes," Danica added, "maybe we just want to get the most out of each twenty-four hours. Why spend too much of it sleeping?"

"I don't think I need my beauty sleep anymore," Jakob said.

"Did you ever get any?" asked Danica.

"You've got to get up pretty oily in the morning . . . " Jakob said this in English. "Did I tell you about what happened with my brother when he first lived in America?"

Danica didn't say anything if she had heard, and Ehmet certainly hadn't.

"When he first arrived he lived with a distant cousin of ours, Louie, who had been in America for many years. They lived in a place called Brooklyn. My brother was just learning English, and he learned mostly from conversations with people. In their neighborhood, many people spoke with a strong accent, peculiar to Brooklyn maybe, though my brother didn't know that. He simply learned from what he heard. One evening, practicing his English, he asked cousin Louie to wake him up early the next day, he was going to ride the subway to downtown New York City to interview for a job. In the morning my brother woke up early and found his face covered in oil. 'What is this?' he asked Louie. 'Oil,' said Louie. 'You asked me to wake you up oily!' My brother had been saying the word 'early' as he had heard people in the neighborhood say it. It sounded like 'oily.' Louie was a joker, you never knew what to expect from him."

"What happened to him?" Ehmet asked.

"He died an old man," said Jakob. "He always had a joke, even up to the end."

"And you, do you have more jokes?" Danica asked Jakob.

"I hope so," answered Jakob. "Also breakfast. Here."

● ● ●

When they had finished eating, Jakob asked Ehmet if he would help him with a few repairs around the farm. Before starting, Ehmet tried to phone his father and grandparents. Still there were no responses.

"Come on," said Jakob, "let's get busy. I know it's disappointing, but fretting about it won't help. We'll try again later."

First was a repair on the chickens' home. Jakob had built a coop with a sheet of plastic in the roof as a skylight. "Chickens like light. They need twelve hours of light a day to want to lay eggs." He had rigged the door to their coop with a contraption of weights and pulleys so that the chickens could hop on a pedal to open it or close it. Hop on the pedal to release the weight, which pulled a rope over a pulley, which opened the door. "Their own private door system." With that door the coop, built on stilts, was fairly safe from predators. But some animal, "possibly a fox," had torn its way through the fence that surrounded the coop and sent the chickens squawking and flapping around the pen a couple of nights ago. Jakob had made a temporary repair then, and wanted to rebuild the enclosure more permanently. He and Ehmet stretched wire fencing and nailed boards to repair it until the two of them thought it would be difficult for invaders to find a way through.

Just outside the fence was a wooden-frame box, covered with wire mesh on all sides except the bottom, which was open. "Know what that is?" Jakob asked.

Ehmet had no idea.

"A chicken machine."

"A chicken machine?"

"Yes. You see how the soil inside the pen is loose from all of the chicken scratching? Many people think chickens are not so smart, but they have their own chicken smarts—they are very efficient. Somehow they find every plant, tiny seed, and root to eat. Not one plant grows inside their enclosure."

Ehmet had not thought about it but it was true, not even a scraggly new sprout was growing inside the chickens' pen.

"This is how it, or the chickens, works." Jakob placed the wire-mesh box in a garden that during the season had been filled with vegetable plants, and that now, after the harvest, had gone to weeds and remains of summer plants. Jakob picked two chickens out of their pen; each chicken had a name—Mambo and Tango—and placed them in the wire-mesh box, the open side facing the earth. The chickens immediately set to scratching, sending dirt flying, nosing their beaks through the soil to devour all of the plant matter they encountered with delectable side dishes of choice insects. Soon they had cleared the patch of earth under the mesh frame so that all that remained were two chickens and loose, freshly turned soil. "That's it. Ready for planting next spring. We just move the machine, and the chickens are on to the next spot."

The rest of the day Jakob and Ehmet repaired the roof of a shed, replacing shingles that would no longer keep the rain and snow out. Sitting on the roof, Ehmet could see across the neighboring farms and countryside, back across the forest to the mountain ridge, seemingly distant in time and space, where he had yesterday crossed the invisible border, a border he now tried to draw in his mind between this and that. He felt again that he could breathe deeply of the crisp, autumn air and relax; the ongoing tension of fleeing, needing full senses alert to possible dangers, easing here. This was an oasis, palms or no.

Jakob was spry enough to gingerly ride the roof, too. Periodically one or the other of them would descend the ladder to get materials—shingles or nails, and move the chicken machine to a new spot adjacent to the area already cleared. By afternoon the chickens had cleared a significant part of the garden. Ehmet was certain his grandparents would like a chicken machine for their yard. He tried to phone them and his father at lunchtime and at intervals throughout the day. In the evening he tried again to no avail.

After dinner the three of them, particularly Ehmet, were quieter than the day before.

"What are you thinking?" Danica asked as Ehmet warmed by the fireplace.

"That I'll still go to my grandparents' house . . . tomorrow. You've been nice. Really. I like being here, I . . . could easily stay."

"And we'd be glad for you to," Danica assured.

"I need to find out what's going on. There's been no fighting where they live as far as I know. They should be there." Ehmet had told them about his grandparents' place.

"Yes, that area's been pretty peaceful from what we hear, too," said Danica. "But don't you want to wait to contact them first?"

"I've been trying, we've been trying. I need to see."

"But if they are not there . . . "

"I know where a key is. I'd be able to stay there."

"We would be happy if you would stay with us until you can contact someone," said Jakob. "We understand though, that you've been on the way to them, your family, for some time. It's natural you are anxious to get there. We are really not far, maybe a couple hours driving. From our village there is a bus that can take you directly to where they live."

"So you'll show me where I can catch the bus?"

"If that is what you want."

"It is."

TWENTY-FIVE

On the Bus

In many ways it was harder for Ehmet to leave than it would have been to stay. He liked it here, liked these people. However, Ehmet was being pulled by the possibilities of his family and propelled by the losses. In the morning he performed what had become the ritual of trying to contact people, and when he could not, packed his backpack once again.

"You are ready?" Jakob asked.

"Yes, as ready as I am going to be," Ehmet answered.

They rode, the three of them, into the village on a tractor. Like a number of people in the countryside, Jakob and Danica did not have a car. The vehicles they had were the most utilitarian: useful for the work they did. For long-distance travel they used other alternatives, like buses, if they were available. In Croatia, the fighting no longer penetrated all areas of the country, was concentrated more in certain border areas, and buses still ran up and down the coast and in some of the interior. In Bosnia, where bus service had ceased, Ehmet had seen families fleeing the fighting, chugging along the roads with their belongings piled high on tractors or in farm trailers towed behind.

Jakob drove, and Danica and Ehmet sat on a board rigged as a bench behind him. Even if they had all wanted to, taking the tractor to his grandparents' house would have meant many uncomfortable hours of travel. The tractor was not rapid transportation; it took a quarter of an hour to get to the village a few miles from the farm. Several people waved as they passed, and when they entered the village it was clear from the way people addressed them that Danica and Jakob were well known.

Danica and Jakob offered to buy Ehmet's ticket. He insisted he had plenty of money to pay his passage. But while Ehmet was digging out the bills, Jakob managed to turn to the small window and pay for the ticket.

It felt odd to be in the village, Ehmet had been in hiding so long. He tried to look inconspicuous while waiting for the bus, leaning against a wall with his backpack stuffed by his legs. Jakob and Danica waited for the bus with him, deflecting questions from villagers about Ehmet with the simple and not particularly revealing response that he was a friend who had stopped for a visit on his way to see his grandparents. When pressed for further specifics, Danica and Jakob immediately moved on to other people they "needed to talk with." Someone asked him his name. Ehmet reached for a Croat one. He grabbed "Ivan," his friend's name, a name friendly both to Ehmet and Croats, he thought.

"Good idea about the name," said Jakob when the visitors had passed. "Some people would be fine about you, about Bosnians, here. But not everyone. This is a small place. No need for everyone to know what they do not need to know. Do you have identification with you?"

"Yes," said Ehmet. He had his student- and picture-ID cards.

"Don't show them unless you have to."

"Yes," added Danica. "If people don't know which side of the fence you are on, it is hard to be on the wrong side."

When the bus was ready to pull out, Danica and Jakob hugged Ehmet.

"You know you are always welcome with us," said Danica. He thanked them.

"It's not far away," said Jakob. "Call if you need anything, anything at all, and come back whenever you want. Good luck."

Ehmet found a window seat and watched the countryside fly by. Riding was certainly different than walking, and Ehmet was glad to be covering ground so quickly. Yet he missed the smells of fields and forests, the sounds of animals and water, the sensations of wind on his face that he had grown accustomed to while walking. Thoughts rolling, he little noticed people getting on and off the bus until a young boy and his mother sat down near him. He looked at them and then turned away. His mother's absence swept him in waves, drew him with the strongest rip current. Looking out the window, just riding, he momentarily managed to banish guilt and allowed himself to be glad to be alive.

When the bus passed through villages and towns, Ehmet was pleased to see people casually going about the ordinary business of the day, not harried by gunfire and fighting. The faces of these people reflected the lack of danger and he smiled when he saw a boy throwing a stick for his dog to retrieve, the kind of ordinary act that was exceptional in the turmoil Ehmet had grown accustomed to. From a bus seat ahead of him a baby peered expectantly over the shoulder of the grandfather holding it. To sit in his own grandparents' living room, to hear the tones of voices he was familiar with, to smell his grandmother's stuffed cabbage cooking, to know the path from the house to the garden, to find an old board in a tree where he had once built a tree house, would be great and desirable treasures. He was tired of being constantly on guard, constantly expecting the unexpected, and longed for what he already knew. He wondered how he would tell his grandparents about his mother's death.

He pictured his grandparents, their house, and the garden behind overflowing with bean plants climbing pole pyramids, tomatoes twining trelisses, even melons in jars. That was a trick he had learned from them: melon in a jar. After the growing season the pantry, a walk-in closet next to their kitchen, would be filled with a flashy rainbow array of bottles—fruits and vegetables they had preserved. Batches of green beans sat next to popping, red tomatoes, orange beets adjoined yellow, pickled cabbage, purple cherries glowed next to light, green-skinned, candied pears. And then there were the melons, a single whole melon in each large jar, his grandparents' novelty.

Each melon filled the glass globe that contained it and was much bigger than the jar's mouth, so could not have been stuffed in. The trick was to place the melon into the jar early in the season when it was just a small, round, green bud. When it grew to fill the jar it was taken off the vine. If you let it grow too long, the expanding melon would burst the glass container. Ehmet's grandparents poured a brew of sweet pickling liquid into the jars with the melons. The end result of the process was candied melons that could be eaten throughout the year, a tasty and unusual food. Getting the melons out of the jars was as tricky as getting them in; they had to be cut with a long-bladed knife while in the jar and the melon slices could then be pulled out.

His grandparents were always experimenting, growing unusual fruits and vegetables in vast quantities, enough to pick and eat daily, to prepare feasts when Ehmet and his family had visited, with a bounty they also gave freely to neighbors. They liked to surprise people. Ehmet decided he would surprise them by building a chicken machine. Walking in, his grandmother was likely to offer Ehmet a glass of the homemade yogurt she made by filling glasses with milk, adding a teaspoon of starter culture from a previous batch, and letting the mix sit for days in a warm spot until it became thick, velvety yogurt. Even that sounded good right now, with its smooth texture and its slightly acidic taste.

These were not thoughts or feelings he had often permitted himself to have on his journey, they were an extravagance that he now stuffed away again, with only a small, hopeful portion poking out.

When the bus eased to a halt for a brief rest stop, Ehmet tugged his backpack loose from beneath his feet and hopped from his ride into the café next door.

It had been so long since he had been able to do something in public as ordinary as get a bit of food or drink in a café—this was phenomenal, good as a trip to the amusement park with an unlimited budget. Though his budget was not unlimited, it didn't need to be. The simplest item from the menu would provide a roller coaster–like thrill.

"Pizza and an orange juice," Ehmet requested from the middle-aged woman who ran the place. The smell of the fresh-baked pizza just about knocked him out. He sat on his stool at the counter savoring each bite.

The bus horn beeped, notice that the rest stop had ended. Ehmet paid his bill and dashed back to his ride.

He settled into his seat. Maybe, just maybe, things would be normal now.

◇

TWENTY-SIX

Camp

The bus was slowing when Ehmet awoke. He had dozed off. He looked out the window to see a group of uniformed Croat soldiers, one with his arm up, signaling the bus to stop.

"What's going on?" he leaned and asked the old man sitting in front of him.

"Checkpoint," said the old man. "They move them around to different places, try to catch smugglers. Or refugees."

Ehmet hadn't expected any checkpoints this far from the border. He sweated.

Two soldiers stepped up into the bus. The first nodded to the driver, then said to the passenger in seat one, "Papers?"

No one said a word as the soldier moved up the aisle scrutinizing each identity card and document, glancing back and forth between the papers and those who handed them to him. The other soldier stood behind him, a shadow sentinel with his rifle. Ehmet debated with himself about what he should do when they got to his seat, until they reached the only other unaccompanied man on the bus, a young man who looked to be in his early twenties, a few rows ahead of Ehmet.

"Papers?" the soldier repeated. Ehmet could see the young man turn his hands up empty, while saying something that Ehmet could not hear. "No papers then?" the soldier said. The young man shook his head no.

"Up," the soldier said. The young man stood up, and the second soldier nudged him off the bus with the butt of his rifle. Ehmet watched as some of the soldiers waiting by the bus hustled the young man into a nearby building.

By the time the soldier got to him, Ehmet had pulled his documents out from where he had hidden them underneath his shirt. He hoped he could talk his way through.

"Papers?" The soldier stared. "Bosnian, eh?"

"I'm on my way to see my grandparents. They're Croatian."

The soldier studied Ehmet's papers some more, and handed them back. Ehmet sighed in relief as the soldier stepped to the seat behind, and kept working his way to the back of the bus.

When he had finished checking everyone on the bus, the soldier strode back down the aisle toward the front. He stopped by Ehmet's seat. "Up."

"But I—" Ehmet started.

"Up," the soldier repeated firmly, for emphasis placing a hand on the pistol he was wearing on his belt.

Ehmet stood up.

"Bring your things," the soldier said.

Ehmet picked up his pack and glanced around. Everyone was staring straight ahead as if they did not see him, the soldier, or what was happening. Only the old man in the seat in front of him gave Ehmet a look as he passed following the soldier. It was a look of concern, Ehmet thought, mouth stretched thin-lipped and downturned.

Once Ehmet and the soldier had stepped off the bus, Ehmet watched it pull away. The soldier had told the driver to go, then led him to the same building into which the soldiers had taken the other young man.

Inside, a soldier was on the phone. He stared at Ehmet while continuing to talk. Ehmet could see the young man from the bus being questioned in an adjoining room. The door closed. The soldier accompanying Ehmet took him into another room. "Sit down."

A couple of chairs and a small, wooden table were the only things in the bare-walled room. Ehmet chose the closest chair, and set his pack beside him. The soldier sat in the other chair, pulled a blank piece of paper from a drawer in the table, and clicked a ballpoint ready to write. "So, your grandparents?" the soldier said, and continued questioning.

Ehmet proceeded to tell him where his Croatian grandparents lived, that they had moved to the village to retire a few years ago, that his mother had been born in Croatia, was Croatian. When the soldier asked how he could contact Ehmet's parents, Ehmet told him that would not be possible, that his mother had died and he didn't know where his father was at the moment.

"Okay then, how will we get in touch with your grandparents?"

Besides their address, Ehmet gave the soldier their phone number, though with the warning that he had not been able to reach them there recently.

The soldier leaned across the table and called out to the soldier who had been on the phone when they walked in, "Igor!"

Igor stepped into the room.

"This kid has Croatian grandparents," Ehmet's questioner said.

"Every refugee piling into Croatia has Croatian family these days," Igor said.

"Here's their number," said the questioner, handing the paper to Igor.

"Okay, okay," said Igor, carrying the number back to his telephone post.

Ehmet could see him dialing, then waiting. He repeated the process a couple of times. The soldier who had been questioning Ehmet tapped his pen on the table absently. Ehmet clutched his backpack and hoped.

"No answer!" Igor called in to them. The soldier sitting opposite Ehmet squinted at the ceiling as if looking for an answer.

"I'm sure they'll be back soon. I know how to get to their house, I can get there on my own," Ehmet said.

"Look, kid. We can't let every Bos . . . every kid wander around the countryside right now."

"But . . . "

"That's the way it is. Sorry. We'll try your grandparents again later." The soldier got up and left the room to join Igor.

Periodically Ehmet heard vehicles pull up outside. Soldiers would leave the building and come back in. Every once in a while Igor would dial a phone number that Ehmet hoped was his grandparents. But Igor did not have any conversations with them. Nor did anyone speak further to Ehmet. After a couple of hours his backside was sore from sitting, and Ehmet got up and wandered around the small room.

In midafternoon, the soldier who had questioned Ehmet returned. "We can't get hold of your grandparents."

"There's these other people I know," Ehmet said, telling him about Jakob and Danica.

"They family?"

"Not exactly."

"Family only. We can only release you to a family member."

"But they'll be glad to . . . "

"If they're not family, it's a big deal. Might take awhile to make that official, get papers."

"A while?"

"Weeks. Months, maybe. Meanwhile, we'll get you to a refugee camp. They've got people there who can help you find your family."

"A camp?"

"You can't stay here," said the soldier, and walked back to Igor's desk.

Almost another hour passed. The questioner returned with a young soldier that Ehmet hadn't seen before. "He'll get you to the camp," the older soldier said, indicating the younger.

They walked past the room where the other bus passenger had been taken earlier in the day. The door was open again, and Ehmet could see his fellow passenger hunched over a desk, head down, cradled in crossed arms.

"Is he going, too?" the young soldier asked the older.

"Nope. When we figure out who he really is, we'll figure out what to do with him."

Ehmet and the young soldier climbed into a small sedan with military insignia on the side and a bar of blue lights on the top.

The young soldier driving Ehmet to the camp was not a talker. He stared ahead at the road, and didn't respond to Ehmet's attempts at conversation. He was doing his duty quietly. Ehmet looked out the window at the passing fields and villages he would not be stopping in.

When they had been driving about half an hour, they arrived at a checkpoint with a huge, metal-beam gate across the road to block any traffic, and armed soldiers at either end.

"This is it," said the young soldier.

"I don't see the camp," said Ehmet.

"It's not far," said the soldier. "They'll get you there." He uncurled a finger from the steering wheel and pointed toward the other soldiers. "This is as far as I go." For the first time, he turned and looked Ehmet in the eyes. "If you have any valuables hidden on you, keep them that way. You'll probably get shaken down at the camp, too."

"By the people who work there?"

"Not likely. Maybe other refugees." The young soldier began rolling down his car window, and pulled over to the end of the gate nearest a small building that served as a guardpost.

A soldier who had been leaning on the end of the gate, smoking a cigarette, peered into the car. "Another Bosnian?"

"Yes," said the driver.

"We'll take him," said the cigarette-smoking soldier with a smile, pulling open the car door on Ehmet's side.

"Good luck," the driver said to Ehmet. He sounded like he meant it.

Ehmet watched the car pull away. "Welcome," said the cigarette soldier, leaning back on his gate and smiling. "Take him to Captain," he said to a young soldier who was nearby, unsteadily cradling a submachine gun. Ehmet started to walk toward him. He, like the driver, was not much older than Ehmet, but this soldier was not calm and straight ahead—he wriggled with fear.

When Ehmet had walked to within a few feet the young soldier barked, "Stop!" He raised his submachine gun to point at Ehmet's chest. "Let me see your hands!"

The young soldier took steps toward Ehmet. "Come with me!" Ehmet could see into the dark hole of the barrel. It was as bad having someone nervous holding a gun as someone angry, Ehmet thought.

The young soldier trailed Ehmet to the small building at the other side of the gate.

At the door of the building the nervous soldier stopped and knocked. "Wait," he implored, keeping the gun pointed at Ehmet. Through a window in the door Ehmet could see a heavyset soldier with salt-and-pepper gray hair, sitting at a desk. He waved them in. The young soldier prodded the gun into Ehmet's back. Behind the desk the old soldier sat rumpled. His hair was disheveled and he needed a shave. He appeared to have been drinking for days. A sour smell of alcohol permeated the air in a mist when he spoke.

"What have we here?" To Ehmet's relief he laughed when he said it. Perhaps he was a good-natured, not a mean, drunk. With the desk-sitter now in charge, the nervous young soldier relaxed and let his gun sag. The old soldier stared at Ehmet. "So, you're a refugee?"

"I'm trying to get to my grandparents."

Ehmet's first impression of the old soldier was quickly altered. "Do you have any money?"

Ehmet knew that question in this context had only one likely meaning. Whatever money they discovered he had would soon be in the hands of the soldiers.

Sounds of a truck motor outside distracted the soldiers, who craned to see. Ehmet stalled, turning his head to look, too.

A knock on the door gave him a break. It was the cigarette-smoking soldier, accompanying a man in a white, nylon jacket. The two walked past Ehmet to the desk. On the back of the white jacket was sewn a large, red cross. The rumpled soldier treated the man in a familiar way, still smiling. "Good to see you."

The man in the white jacket did not seem so pleased.

"Do you have your fees for passage?"

Without speaking, the man in the white jacket extracted a small pile of money, mark notes, from a pocket and set them on the desk. The rumpled soldier counted the bills. "Not enough."

"But that's what it cost last time."

"The fee's gone up."

"We can't afford . . . "

"You want to get to the camp, the fee's gone up."

The man in the white jacket begrudgingly took a few more notes from his wallet. "You're going to make it too expensive for us to get through."

"I'm sure you'll figure out something," the rumpled soldier admonished. He looked over at Ehmet. "You could do us a favor and take him with you to the camp. Save us the gas." He turned to the cigarette-smoking soldier. "And you ride with them, too, make sure this kid doesn't decide to take any walks."

Ehmet wasn't thrilled at the prospect of this ride. But if he didn't get out of here now in one piece, he was afraid he might not at all.

"We need to ask him some questions," said the rumpled soldier.

"So ask," the man in the white jacket said.

"Umm, where are you from?"

"Sarajevo."

"Do you have any identification?"

Ehmet showed a card.

"Bosnian. Family?"

"I'm trying to find them."

"Are you a member of any armed forces?"

"No."

"We'll have to search you." The cigarette-smoking soldier reached into Ehmet's pockets and pat-searched him from neck to shoes. It was more of a slap search with the force he used. Ehmet hoped they would not make him take off his shoes or strip off his clothes. Meanwhile, the young soldier dumped Ehmet's belongings out of his backpack. With the pots and pans, clothes, and other meager possessions Ehmet carried, he looked like what he was, a bedraggled traveler.

The white-jacketed driver of the truck was getting impatient. "Look, he's a kid, says he's a refugee. What more do you need to know?"

"Not much, I guess," said the rumpled soldier at a loss for excuses to hold Ehmet further with the white-jacketed man a witness. "You can go, then," he said.

"Let's go," the truck driver said to Ehmet.

Ehmet restuffed his things into the backpack and hurried from the building with the driver, out of hearing of the soldiers.

"They aren't all like that. Some of them mean well," the driver said to Ehmet once the two of them were in the front seat of the truck.

"Yeah," said Ehmet.

"But with these guys here, everyone's someone to shake down. They've made me pay more each time I try to pass."

"You come through a lot?"

"Lately every day. A shipment just came in to the port at Split and this is our only truck. Back and forth. Yesterday, today, tomorrow. There are a lot of people at the camp."

Ehmet was about to ask the driver more. But the cigarette-smoking soldier climbed up into the truck cab with them, the driver shifted the truck into gear, and they lurched forward.

The closer they got to the camp, the more a worried gnawing in Ehmet's stomach chewed at the rest of him. As they approached, Ehmet saw dozens and dozens of tents set on wooden platforms in rows, surrounded by a high, barbed-wire-topped fence. At the corners of the fence were wooden guard towers, each manned by a uniformed soldier. More soldiers, all in the same kind of uniform as those who had searched Ehmet before, stopped the truck at a gate. One approached the vehicle. "Hey, Franjo," he said to the cigarette-smoking soldier, who hopped down out of the truck.

"And him?" The gate guard nodded at Ehmet.

"Bosnian. For you," said the cigarette smoker, and walked over to talk with some of the other soldiers.

The truck driver handed the gate guard a sheaf of official-looking papers, plenty of lines of small print and signatures with a few rubber-stamped seals, which the soldier leafed through and handed back unceremoniously.

"Go ahead," said the guard.

The driver pulled to the front door of a simple, wood-plank building, the only structure besides the tents that Ehmet could see in the camp. Notices pinned to a bulletin board next to the door flapped in the breeze.

The two of them entered the building.

A woman busily writing at a desk glanced up, then back to her writing.

A young man, neatly dressed, got up from behind a desk where he had been shuffling papers and said in English to the driver, "Stefan. Glad you made it."

"I am too, Erik." They shook hands.

"You brought someone with you?"

"Had to. He's looking for his family."

"Not the only one. Do you speak English?" Erik addressed Ehmet.

"Some."

"Where are you from?"

"Sarajevo."

"Hmmm. Maybe you'll find someone you know here. Maralisa is out doing interviews. She'll talk to you. You can wait in here while Stefan and I unload the truck." Erik started out, then turned to Ehmet. "You may as well help, too. Okay?"

"Sure." Ehmet was glad to keep busy rather than just sit and wait.

◇

TWENTY-SEVEN

Waiting

Unloading did not take long. The back of the truck didn't hold a huge number of boxes and bundles. Most of the load was bundles of blankets, and some boxes labeled with drug names and symbols of medical supplies.

When they had finished stacking the goods in the warehouse, Erik carefully attached a huge padlock to the outside of the solid, warehouse door and yanked on it to make sure it was locked.

"Have a seat," Erik said to Ehmet when they were back in the office. "Maralisa should return soon." He motioned to one of the few pieces of unoccupied furniture in the bare room, a folding, metal chair like Ehmet's family had for when guests came over to visit and there were more people than pieces of furniture.

The driver handed the last of his paperwork to Erik. "See you tomorrow then."

"Good luck," he said to Ehmet with a wave on his way out.

"Thanks." Ehmet sat in the chair and waited.

He waited for a half hour or so, watching the two people working at their desks. Neither took much note of Ehmet. They were preoccupied with their tasks. Erik kept filling out forms and typing on a computer keyboard. The other, a woman perhaps in her twenties, did paperwork and talked on the phone periodically. Ehmet could not understand much of what she was talking about; a lot of it related to numbers.

Then he remembered Milan's book. It was a welcome diversion. Ehmet had almost finished the story when a middle-aged woman appeared through the doorway.

"Maralisa," said Erik. "This young man needs to be interviewed."

"I'm exhausted," Maralisa said to Erik in English. Then she said to Ehmet in Croatian, "Pull your chair over here." She sat at the only remaining desk in the room.

Ehmet carried his chair over to the desk. "I'm looking for my grandparents, my aunt and uncle, maybe my father," he blurted.

"We'll try to help you. First I need to ask you some things." She proceeded to ask him a series of questions: his name and where he was from, his age, parents' and other family members' names, and where he thought they might be, and a bit about his journey and where he had been recently. Most of his answers she wrote down on a form. "So these are the people you are hoping to find?" She read off the names. He agreed. She highlighted their names with a yellow marker.

"Take this over to Erik." She handed Ehmet the form.

Erik compared the highlighted names to lists he brought up on the computer screen. "I'm checking to see if any of these names are on our lists of people we have in the camp."

Ehmet started to sweat, the moisture soaking through the back of his shirt, sticking it to the chair.

"I'm sorry, I don't see that any of these people are here. Which would be the best phone numbers and addresses to use to try and contact people?" Ehmet marked them. Erik handed the form to the young woman who had been on the phone at the other desk. "Ana, can you try these?"

Ana dialed numbers from the form. Ehmet sweated profusely, hoping to hear her say "hello" to someone each time she tried a new number. All he heard was her dialing and redialing.

"We should get you registered," said Erik. He pulled out yet another form.

"Registered?"

"To stay here for now."

"Maybe I'll be able to find them somewhere else. My grandparents will get home, I'll meet them . . . "

"You want to leave?"

"Yes."

"I'm sorry, we can't just let you go. You are thirteen. We have to release you into the care of someone. When we get in touch with one of your family members . . . "

After all the care he had taken making decisions to stay free in his journey, Ehmet felt the weight of being in the camp. Before, however difficult it had been, he was able to move, to search, to travel some portion of the earth's surface. Now he was about to become buried in paperwork. He was trapped.

"Look," said Erik, "we'll keep trying to reach someone for you, though it may take a little time. We have a lot of people to try and track down."

"I'll show you where you can stay," said Maralisa. "We have a number of people here from Sarajevo. Maybe you'll find someone you know."

Ehmet strapped his pack on his sticky back and followed Maralisa. He carried his jacket rather than wearing it, even though the afternoon air was chilling. He was trying to cool down. Maralisa led him through the tent rows. In cracks between the canvas flaps that served as tent doors, Ehmet caught sliced views of people moving within—a mother stroking a baby's forehead, a couple of toddlers racing in circles, an old woman packing what might have been clothes.

A few people passed carrying water buckets, a sight that reminded Ehmet of life in Sarajevo. Several young kids raced by. Occasionally in the intersections of tent rows, small groups of teens and adults stood talking in subdued voices. Some appeared well-fed and neat, others were gaunt and disheveled. Most said hello or lifted hands to acknowledge Maralisa as they passed. Ehmet got looks of assessment, curiosity, or indifference.

"You'll be here," Maralisa said, stopping by a tent. "Hello," she called through the flaps and pulled one aside so she and Ehmet could enter.

Following her in, Ehmet saw that the only person inside was an old man sitting on his cot, his back propped by a cloth bundle. He set down the newspaper he had been reading. "I'm looking for some good news," he said smiling. "Doesn't matter that it's last week's does it?"

"Good news is good news," said Maralisa. "And to answer your next question, we haven't heard from your son again yet, but I'm hopeful we will soon."

"Me, too, I'm hopeful," said the old man. "Who is this?"

"His name is Ehmet. Can we put him in the empty bed?" Four cots, each canvas stretched on a metal frame to form a bed, were the only furniture in the tent. The old man sat on one, two had clothes and other belongings on or under them, the fourth was empty.

"I don't see why not," said the old man. He extended his right hand to Ehmet to shake. "Welcome to the bachelor tent. One of them, anyway. I'm Marko."

Ehmet shook hands.

"Marko will tell you how things work at the camp, no?"

"Certainly," said Marko.

"You can come and take a turn with the telephone tomorrow morning, try to find your people," Maralisa said to Ehmet as she flapped out of the tent.

"That will be a challenge," said Marko, "using the phone. You'll have to wait in line. Waiting in lines is the main thing I can tell you about this place, waiting in lines and just waiting. It's not so bad though. You get to share a tent with me. Well, me and these two."

A boy a little younger than Ehmet, perhaps twelve, burst into the tent. "Hey, she was telling the truth, we do have a new guy here." He was energetic and animated. The boy reminded Ehmet of Ali.

"This is Armin," said Marko. "And that's Goran." A much older, larger boy hulked into the tent. He was big-framed and heavy, with a turned-down look on his face. Ehmet guessed he was in his late teens.

"So who are you?" Armin asked.

"Ehmet."

"Where you from?" Ehmet could see this smaller kid, Armin, wasn't going to give up easily—he was all over the place, bouncing around the tent, persistent. "Where you from?" he repeated.

"Sarajevo." Ehmet didn't see the point of trying to keep that secret here, everyone was from different places, and if he hoped to find anyone who might be from Sarajevo he knew he had a better shot if he spread that information.

"Hey, Goran is from Sarajevo, right, Goran?" Goran nodded in agreement.

"Where did you live in Sarajevo?" Ehmet asked Goran, hoping he would open up.

"The Old City." Goran did not elaborate, and Ehmet did not press. The Old City was the area of Sarajevo his father had gone to before losing touch. Gone, maybe like his mother. Perhaps there were things Goran didn't want to talk about either.

Armin continued. "You don't know each other, huh? Hey, Goran, remember those other guys we met from Sarajevo?" Goran nodded again. "Maybe you'll know somebody. We could show you where they live . . . where they are staying," he corrected himself. "You want to meet 'em?"

"Yes," Ehmet responded. He picked up his backpack: He had set it next to the cot he was supposed to use.

"You don't have to take that with us," Armin told him.

"That's all right," said Ehmet, shouldering the pack. "I'm used to having it with me." That was true, it had become part of him, was most often a hump on his back and had usually been no farther away from him than his arm's length over the past weeks. What he did not say was that he was also taking it because he did not yet accept this as his home. He was not ready to settle in.

The three of them navigated the rows of tents. All looked similar from the outside, cream colored, straight-walled, peak-roofed. Ehmet knew there were more distinctive worlds within. Several tents had laundry hung to dry on the outside supporting ropes. Otherwise it was easy to lose track of where you were— there were few landmarks, just small numbers posted on sticks at the ends of rows.

Armin and Goran seemed to know their way around. Armin did, anyway. He chattered and guided them to turn right here, turn left there, and at one point shoved Ehmet to dodge with him between tents when they saw a motley group of young men approaching with none-too-friendly expressions.

Within minutes they had arrived at a tent that looked no different than the rest to Ehmet, but that Armin and Goran somehow recognized. Tent recognition appeared to be a learned skill. "This is one of them, right, Goran?" Goran did his job and nodded again.

"Hello, it's me, Armin, the kid from yesterday. Remember me?" Armin called through the flaps at the tent entryway. It seemed likely that Armin would be remembered. If not, he would remind you.

It was weird not having a door to knock on. A couple of canvas flaps, a thin layer of cloth was all that walled the people within from the people outside. A boy about Armin's age came to the entryway and pulled a flap out of the way to see. "Hey."

"Hey," Armin answered. They spoke the same language.

"Hey," the kid in the tent said again.

"This new guy is looking for people he knows. He's from Sarajevo. You are too, right?"

"Right." The boy squinted at Ehmet. "But I don't know him."

"Is anybody else in your family here?"

"Mom, Dad, Natalia!" the boy turned and called over his shoulder.

"Let them in," a man's voice said.

Ehmet, Armin, and Goran followed the boy into the tent. "Better to talk in here," the man who had spoken before said. He was middle-aged and bulky, bigger than Goran, and soft spoken. "Which of you is looking for people?"

Ehmet thought Armin and Goran might be as well, but it was him now. "Me."

"You other kids don't have to stay," said the man. With the boy who had greeted them, plus Armin, Goran, and Ehmet, there were a lot of boys in the small tent.

Armin was more than ready to bounce off. "Come on," he said to the boy his age, "let's get outside for a while." The boy looked at his parents.

"It's okay," said his mother. "But stay nearby. And you know, be careful."

Armin and the boy went running. Goran stood there alone, wriggling uncomfortably. "I'll meet you back at our tent," he mumbled to Ehmet, and took his leave.

Sitting on a cot near the man were the boy's mother and a girl about Ehmet's age—the boy had called her Natalia. The man and woman asked Ehmet the names of all of the people he was looking for. Ehmet told them. They didn't know any of them, or anything about them, except Ehmet's father. "Does he write for the newspaper?" the woman asked. She remembered reading articles he had written. "He's a good writer."

Natalia had been listening. So far she hadn't said anything though Ehmet was hoping she would. There was something about her beyond the fact that he hadn't seen many girls his age in some time. She seemed thoughtful, and in a way that he couldn't explain, at peace.

"What school did you go to?" she asked.

Ehmet thought at first that was just what any teenager might ask another if there were no other obvious touch-points for communication. But when he told her the name of his school, he found she had a particular reason for asking.

"I know a boy who went to that school."

"What's his name?"

"Milan."

TWENTY-EIGHT

Friends

Ehmet was stunned. Then elation lifted him from the trap he thought he had entered today. "Milan?" There was only one Milan who had gone to his school as far as Ehmet knew.

"Yes. You know him?" Natalia asked.

"I think so," Ehmet affirmed.

"You want me to take you to him?"

"Natalia . . . " said her mother. "I don't want you just wandering around."

"I know where his family is staying."

"I don't mean that."

"Mom. I'll be fine. I'm not a kid."

"Not just the two of you alone." Her mother eyed Ehmet with suspicion. He hadn't thought of himself as a danger.

"I guess we can't keep you cooped in here for months at a time," said Natalia's father. "You'll have to bring your brother along."

"I'm used to that. All right."

From the entryway of the tent, her father whistled to the outside, a distinctive low tone then a high-pitched trill. When there was no response, he whistled again.

His son came flying into the tent, followed by Armin.

"What?"

"We want you to go with your sister. She's going to take this young man to his friend. Then you come right back with her, okay?"

"He'll go with us, too?" the boy pointed at Armin.

"That's fine."

"Right back here," said Natalia's mother. "No monkey business."

Natalia guided the three boys. Armin and her brother rocketed like pinballs around Natalia and Ehmet, occasionally returning to the center where the two teens walked.

"So how do you know Milan?" Ehmet asked Natalia.

"We met in a line. He was behind me. Usually you have to wait a long time around here. Sometimes waiting is not so bad. He was fun to talk to."

Ehmet wondered if Milan had worked hard to get behind Natalia in line, or it had just happened that way.

"What about you?" she asked him.

"We're best friends."

"Best friends?" She looked incredulous.

"If this is the same Milan. We always have been."

"You're finding your best friend in a camp. That's the golden strand."

"The golden strand?"

"That winds through things. Can't be all bad. Even when you can't see it."

Ehmet was pleased to meet an optimist. He figured he might be due for some good luck. He hoped Milan would be Milan and everything would be okay.

"This is it," Natalia said. "Milan, are you in there?"

"What!" Milan tugged back the tent flaps. He fell backward as if a blast of wind had caught him, then clung to a flap and pulled himself up. "You're kidding! Man what are you doing here?" His shock dissipated and he broke into a grin. "This is incredible!"

"Thought you could lose me, huh?" Ehmet said.

"Right," sang Milan. "And you know Natalia?"

"That kid, Armin, introduced us. Said he knew people from Sarajevo."

Milan was shaking his head, still getting over the stun.

"Aren't you going to invite us in?" Natalia asked.

"Sure, sure. Come in."

"You wait out here," Natalia said to her brother and Armin, who had been buzzing up and down the aisles between tents. They seemed to have a limitless capacity for chasing each other, and were pleased to be able to stay outside and continue chasing. Armin's batteries might ultimately wear down, but it wasn't clear when.

The tent was empty of people other than the three of them, though there was gear around every cot. "What about your family?" Ehmet asked Milan.

"Oh, they're here. Just took my little sister to try and get some medicine. She's had some kind of stomach thing."

"How long have you been in this place?" asked Ehmet.

"A couple of weeks. We left Sarajevo not long after you and your mom. Got out while we still could. My father knew some people who knew some people, you know the . . . guys surrounding the city." Ehmet knew. Milan's father was of Serb background, the ring around the city was a Serb ring. "And he paid. You know that T-shirt my cousin always liked? The one with the rock-and-roll logo? His father said if I gave him the T-shirt, he would loan us two thousand dollars to help get out. I wasn't sure if he was joking or not, so I gave him the T-shirt to make sure. We were in a truck first. In Croatia we took a bus. Then got stuck here. Where have you been?"

"Walking, mostly," Ehmet said.

"Walking?"

"I took a bus, got a couple of rides in Croatia."

"Just you? What about your mom?"

"She . . . she died." Ehmet snapped shut. It was exhausting opening that sore.

Milan rubbed his chin and tried to think of something to say. "Geez. Sorry." The three of them sat in silence.

"I'm sorry," said Natalia. Ehmet felt like the two of them

meant it, and this was the first time he'd been able to really hear that since his mother had died. Other people, Jakob and Danica for instance, had meant it, too, he knew, but he hadn't been able to take it in until now. A solid structure of pain had blocked most of his sensations. Maybe something was changing. He was able to look around, climb the wall rather than bang his head against it.

Milan continued to sit on the edge of his cot, rubbing his chin, then scratching his head. Ehmet knew Milan well enough to know he was trying to sort things out. He wasn't worried about that, he'd hear from him eventually. Next to him on the cot was a book, cover up, pages facedown, open to where Milan had been reading it before Natalia and Ehmet arrived. Milan was a big reader.

"I finished your book. The one you lent me." Ehmet dug into his backpack, lifted the book out, and nudged the pack under the cot with his foot. He felt comfortable leaving it here.

"You've been lugging that around?"

Ehmet assumed Milan meant the book. "It's not that heavy a book. You probably kept half of it."

"Yeah, the good half." It was one of their jokes. Once, when they had both wanted to read a paperback that was falling apart, eack took a few chapters and swapped after reading them.

"Besides, good story. I just finished it. Here."

"Glad you liked it. I'm into this one now. Natalia, do you want to read that one?"

"I'll take it." Books were in short supply in the camp; time was not. "A paperback." Ehmet handed her the book. "I can read while I'm waiting in lines. Then I'll have something to do besides stare at people."

"Sure they are not staring at you?"

"Milan, are you jealous?"

"Maybe."

"That's sweet."

Armin and his friend poked their heads into the tent. "What are you three doing?" teased Natalia's little brother. Armin giggled.

"Talking!" Natalia told him.

"We're supposed to go right back," her little brother said.

"Like you listen to Mom and Dad."

"Oh, sure I do."

"We'll go in a few minutes. I'll call you."

Armin and her little brother disappeared outside again.

"Little kids," said Natalia.

"Lucky we were never like that," said Milan.

"We couldn't have been," said Natalia.

"Sure weren't," added Ehmet. "We did tease Darko, though."

"Hey, he deserved it," said Milan. Ehmet wasn't sure what any-one deserved these days. "Especially after what he did to Mira. Trying to trip her, remember?"

Ehmet remembered. How low could you go?

"You won't believe this. Mira was here."

"Here, in the camp?"

"Yup. Until a few days ago. She didn't stay long. She was going to Mrs. Barisic's."

"Mrs. Barisic's?" Ehmet didn't understand.

"The place Mrs. Barisic helped start for . . . kids without fami-lies. It's on the Istrian Peninsula, you know, near Italy, in a little village. Only part of Croatia where there was no fighting at all. Supposed to be a peaceful place. Kids are even helping build part of it. Something like that. That's what Mira said."

"Build part of it?"

"It's really old, one of those medieval villages. A lot of the buildings were falling down. The kids are helping fix them up. Putting together some new buildings, too."

"How's Mira doing?" Ehmet had to ask.

"Mira, spunky as ever. She's been on her own, too. Came here with a busload of orphans. You know her father got killed when she lost her leg. Something happened to her mother recently. She didn't tell me exactly what."

"So how did she get hooked up with Mrs. Barisic?"

"I guess Mrs. Barisic had given her the address a while ago of the place she's been working on, so Mira could keep in touch. Mira called it 'The Children's Village.'"

"And Mira just went there?"

"Just went there, no. Mira got out of Sarajevo with orphan kids on a special bus convoy. The people who run this camp had set that up. Then Mrs. Barisic came and picked up Mira. They'd already arranged it. Most of the kids who came on that bus are still here."

"You know they don't just let you leave," added Natalia. "Especially if you're not an adult. It's all got to be arranged."

"Yeah, in some ways this camp is like a prison," said Milan.

"I saw all the guards around it," Ehmet said.

"They're to keep us in. Supposed to protect us, too. But they don't want us Bosnians, Serbs, or Muslims, or whatever, out in the Croat countryside. They'll shoot you if you try to escape," said Milan.

"That's happened?" Ehmet asked.

"Not since I've been here. But I heard they did before, shoot at people."

"That's what I heard, too," said Natalia. "At least this is a refugee camp. The people who run it are trying to help. You can get food, medicine. And they will try to help you find a place to resettle. This is a much better situation than what some people have had to face."

"That's true," said Milan. "But it's not the greatest place to be a Serb right now."

"Did those guys jump you again?" Natalia asked.

"Not since the other day. I haven't wanted to say, to tell you either, Ehmet. But I . . . might have to leave. My family is probably getting transferred to a Serb camp."

"Are you still trying to get to Canada?" asked Natalia.

"Yes. Except that could take a long time."

"When?" Ehmet asked.

"It could be months."

"I mean, when is your family getting transferred?"

"Maybe in two days."

TWENTY-NINE

◇

The Fence

After they talked for a while they walked Natalia and her brother back to her family's tent. Armin rushed away to find Goran.

"See you later," Milan and Natalia promised each other.

"You, too," Natalia added to Ehmet as she disappeared into the tent. He was glad to be included.

"We can go get in line for dinner," Milan suggested to Ehmet. "It's early, but if we wait now, we'll be near the front of the line. Won't have to wait later. I guess that's not much of a choice, wait now or wait later, but it's a choice."

"She's cool," said Ehmet.

"Natalia?"

"Yeah."

"You don't have to convince me," said Milan.

"You have something going on with her?"

"I hope so."

"Seems like it," said Ehmet.

"So you want to go get in line?"

"For being in love with Natalia?"

"For dinner, yo-yo." Milan punched him playfully on the arm. "Good to see you."

They dropped by the infirmary, a tent near the office Ehmet had been in earlier, to see what was happening with Milan's little sister and to let his parents know they were headed for the dinner line. Ehmet tried to go in with Milan. They were stopped at the doorway by a guard. "You two sick?"

"No," said Ehmet.

"Just want to see my parents and sister. She's in here with some stomach thing."

"You see them?" The guard held Ehmet outside with his arm and stepped aside to let Milan take a look.

"They're over there," Milan pointed.

"Go in then. Say what you have to say, then out. This is not clinic hours, emergency only. You wait outside," he said to Ehmet.

Ehmet stood in the evening, looking away from the tent and out at the fence, the fence that surrounded all of them.

Milan was back outside within a few moments. "My parents are real glad you got here. They are really sorry about your mom. They'll talk to you soon's they can get out of there. My sister's a little better."

"So what do you want to do?"

"Let's go get in line."

They weren't the first in line, though Milan said it would be another hour before dinner was served. There were about fifty people waiting outside the tent where the food was being prepared. Smells drifted over the crowd and Ehmet could hear the hiss and sizzle of gas stoves. Among the crowd were a number of shockingly thin people.

"What about those guys?" Ehmet whispered to Milan as they approached.

"People escaped from towns, villages. Whole villages got cleared out. I hate to say it. Militias took . . . Muslim guys and boys—villagers, not soldiers—and just shot them. Other people got sent to prison camps, not refugee camps. Tortured, raped people they hadn't killed already, starved people. Some Serbs did that to Croats also. And they say Croats to Serbs and Muslims. Some Muslims have done their damage, too. Everybody can find a reason to get pissed off at everybody else.

"I met a bunch of guys about our age who'd seen most of the men and boys from their village shot. Then they were forced at gunpoint to work for a year like slaves before they escaped. You should have seen them. No. Better you didn't. Thinner than these guys even. They were walking skeletons when they escaped and got here."

This was a world of ghosts. Ehmet decided he couldn't stay for long. He felt walled in with his own memories and those of too many others that were as bad or worse. It was great seeing Milan, but he had found his friend in a dark place.

"How did you manage, walking all that way?" Milan asked.

"I ran, part of it." Ehmet said, trying to deflect. Then he relented and told Milan as much as he could about what had happened to him and his mother on the journey, and how he had gotten this far. His voice was a murmur so the people around wouldn't hear. Though they may have heard such accounts before, this was his life and he was not ready to invite a new group to wander through it.

"Man," said Milan when Ehmet ended his account. "I really am glad you made it here."

The line had built from a small crowd to a milling mass of hundreds of people. Milan's father joined the two of them in line. Grumbles that he was crashing the line erupted from a few of the surrounding people. Milan's father explained that Milan was his son, that his daughter was in the infirmary and was not eating, and showed a blue card that entitled him to get a meal to bring back to his wife who had stayed with her there. The grumblers quieted.

"Ehmet, it's good to see you," said Milan's father. "You can stay with us. I'm really sorry about your mother. She was a wonderful woman." He did not press.

The line did. People crushed forward to get to the food, and the three of them were swept along. When they reached the ladling point in the tent, bowls that Milan's father pulled from his side bag each got filled with a wallop of stew. Flour dumplings floated in the juices of a couple of food groups brewed together, but it smelled decent. With chunks of thick-crusted bread in hand as well, they exited the kitchen tent. Ehmet had been so focused on food lately he was beginning to think becoming a chef would be a good career choice.

Milan's father carried two bowls of food into the infirmary to share with the rest of the family. Milan and Ehmet sat around the corner from the guard, and scooped up mouthfuls of stew with the bread. Looking over the rim of his bowl, Ehmet studied the fence.

◇

THIRTY

Break

The next morning, Ehmet beelined for the office. Milan and his father went along. They encountered a horde of other refugees, all waiting with hopes in—or out—of hand. Morning was the time for the refugees to make phone calls, and otherwise try to get the help of the office staff to contact people. The process was a routine of waiting and filling out forms each day with hopes that the long wait would be punctuated by big news. Months could go by, years, while wheels outside of the fence turned slowly, or as those inside feared, stopped completely. Papers were moved from one desk to another, in and out of the camp. Many refugees made it their daily task to question the staff, to try to prod hard or often enough that their needs might somehow be felt outside the fence. At least not be forgotten.

In Milan's family's case, they hoped to hear from his older sister who had gone to university in Canada, and, with luck, to get papers to enter that country.

Simple math was enough to figure out that with three people helping hundreds, each refugee had just minutes a day to try to find or start another life. Ten minutes maximum for phone call-ing or completing forms, asking or answering questions.

Ehmet waited his turn anxiously while the morning drifted by in a haze of shuffling papers and people.

When his time arrived, he spent the first minutes trying his list of phone numbers. He handed the phone back to Maralisa.

"Couldn't reach anyone?"

"No."

Milan and his father had finished at the next desk and rejoined Ehmet.

"Not good," Milan said.

"We're being transferred," said Milan's father. "To another camp. Leaving in two days. I asked to get that changed or have you come with us."

"I'm sure Ana told you, that's just not possible," said Maralisa. She looked to Ana at the next desk, who nodded. "Your paperwork has been approved, and we can't stop the transfer process now."

"Can't he just come with us?" said Milan.

"Sorry," said Maralisa. "He is not part of your family . . . "

"He is," Milan said.

"Yes, as far as we're concerned, he's family," Milan's father added.

"Not on paper," said Maralisa. "And besides, you're going to a Serb camp. Ehmet might not be welcomed there. You can keep in touch. He can stay here until we get things straightened out."

Ehmet saw his opportunity to leave the camp with Milan's family slipping away. "I have an idea. I know some people near here. There's a place called the Children's Village . . . "

"Yes, I know it. We have sent several orphans there. But you are not an orphan. As far as we know, you still have family. First we have to try to reach them."

"I haven't been able to get in touch with them. I'm like an orphan."

"Look, if we really can't get you reconnected with your family, perhaps we can start the process to get you released to some-where else. But it's not that simple. There's a lot of paperwork to be done, and we need to have time to try to contact your family."

"How much time would that be?"

"Perhaps a month. Maybe more. You can come here every day.

We'll keep trying. Sorry." Maralisa waved for the next person in line to step to the desk. "Next."

Ehmet stepped back, trying to think of something else. All he could think of was that he was trapped.

"Come on, let's take a walk," Milan suggested to Ehmet when they were outside.

The two of them passed the fenced area behind the office, the warehouse where Ehmet had helped unload the truck only yesterday. Until yesterday he had been free to move on his own. Now he was inside, and the immediate prospects for being outside had disappeared. He and Milan continued making a circuit around the camp. Milan tried to cheer Ehmet, to discuss any number of things that in the past would have immediately captured Ehmet's interest. But Ehmet was difficult to reach. While they paced the aisles, Ehmet's head kept turning toward the fence. "I can't stay in this cage."

"Things will get straightened out."

"It's different for you, Milan. You're waiting for something, you're leaving in two days with your family, then maybe going to Canada. Natalia's family is waiting to go to the United States. Me, I'm in total limbo."

"But your father . . . "

"I don't know what's happened with my father."

"Your grandparents, your aunt and uncle. You'll get in touch with your family, you'll get out, one way or the other."

"It's a big mistake, my being here. It's bad not knowing. Sitting around and not knowing, for me that's the worst."

"We're not sitting, we're walking." Milan tried to lighten the conversation.

"However we're doing it, I can't just wait in limbo. I've got to do something more and try to find my family. I dug my way in, I'll dig my way out."

"Digging might take awhile."

"Not if I have wheels."

"Wheels?"

"I'm thinking I could get out the same way I got in. On the truck."

Ehmet explained his plan, as much as he'd figured out, to

Milan. Milan could see that Ehmet not only wanted to leave the camp, he was set on it. Their friendship had helped both of them overcome many obstacles. The fence was a hurdle for Ehmet, and Milan agreed he would help him get over it.

They kept the plan to themselves so no one would have to compromise or cover for Ehmet. If no one knew, no one could tell or try to dissuade him. First step was to get Ehmet's backpack out of the tent without anyone in Milan's family seeing.

They waited until Milan's parents took his sister back to the infirmary for a checkup, and got the pack.

The two of them dodged contact with people, zigzagging between tents as they made their way toward the office. Ehmet was certain that if anyone could read his movements, as you could a bee's, they would know his was a dance of excitement saying "I have a plan for leaving this place." Mrs. Barisic, whose interests in life extended even to insects, had told them how bees did dances with specific movements that communicated to the rest of the hive a variety of messages—how to get from here to there, what was currently going on in the surrounding countryside.

Milan could read him. "Hot Pepper, you are excited."

They stepped between a couple of tents near the front entry gate, where they could see any comings and goings from the camp. They sat and watched for the truck. An hour after Ehmet thought it should have arrived, he started to get edgy. The driver had seemed steady and reliable. He had no reason to say he'd been making daily trips if he hadn't. Milan agreed. He thought he'd noticed the truck every day for the last week and tried to reassure Ehmet that it would show up soon.

More of the early afternoon passed, and they were still waiting. Though they were both now used to time as a shape shifter, not predictable in form or content, both wondered if for some reason it had frozen altogether.

They heard the rumbling of the truck before they saw it.

THIRTY-ONE

Dark

As yesterday, the truck passed through the front gate and pulled up to the front door of the office. The same driver descended from the truck cab and made his way inside. That was Ehmet's cue.

Ehmet bolted from between the tents and slowed to a walk as he reached the truck. He waited by the driver's door, trying to act casual. In a few minutes the driver came out of the office and was ready to reboard the truck. "Hey, kid," he said to Ehmet. "How are things going?"

"Not too bad." Ehmet decided to give a guarded but honest answer. He had planned two possible approaches to leaving in the truck. This conversation was the first. "I really don't think I should be here, that this is the best place to find my family." He revealed only as much of his intent as he felt he could without alarming the driver, in case he had to go with the second option.

"I'm sorry to hear that. I was concerned about bringing you. But the people here will try to help. I'm sure they will. I'm sorry I couldn't help you more."

That was it. The driver wasn't going to offer to get him out of the camp. Ehmet put option two, the backup plan, into gear. "There's not much to do around here. Can I help you . . . "

Erik rounded the truck with two burly men. "All right," he said to the driver. "Let's go."

"Can I help you unload the truck?" blurted Ehmet.

"Not today," said Erik.

"I know what to do," Ehmet insisted. "I did a good job yesterday, right?"

"You did," the driver affirmed.

"Thanks for your help then," Erik said to Ehmet. "But today we're unloading food sacks that weigh more than you do. These guys will help." He nodded toward the two hefty men.

"But . . . " said Ehmet.

"Maybe some other time. Sorry. I don't want you getting hurt." That was Erik's final answer. "Let's go." He turned away and started toward the warehouse with the two men.

The driver got into the truck to maneuver it to the back of the building. "See you, kid. Best of luck." He waved.

Ehmet touched two fingers to his forehead and flashed them in a waving salute. He was crestfallen, yet mustered all his energies to continue appearing relaxed, as if it was no big deal that he could not help unload the truck. He was not about to abandon his effort to leave the camp, and he did not want to tip off anyone other than Milan.

As the truck pulled out of sight around the building, Ehmet walked back to the row of tents where Milan waited.

"What happened?"

"They said I couldn't help unload today. The stuff's too heavy."

"Oh no."

"I have an idea of how I can still do it."

That stubbornness did not surprise Milan. At any rate, he had resolved to help Ehmet. "So what now?"

"I'll go back over there and sneak around the side of the building. If they happen to see me running around with the backpack, they'll probably get wise to what I'm up to. You bring the backpack once I'm there. If they catch you coming over with the pack, just wander toward the tents and I'll take off without it."

"What are you going to do?"

"Get on the truck."

"How?"

"You'll see. If you want, once you give me the pack you could watch from between the tents back near the warehouse. Just don't tell anybody what happens."

"What about Natalia? She'll want to know. She can keep a secret."

"You sure?"

"Yes."

"Well, I wanted to say good-bye to her anyway. So, okay. And your family, too. But not 'til I get out of here. Okay? I'm off. See you."

The two slapped hands.

Ehmet sauntered toward the office as if he were going to enter it. He looked around, and when he was as sure as he could be that no one was watching, he dashed around the corner and hugged close to the wall. He motioned for Milan to join him. Milan sped over from the tents with the backpack.

"Thanks," whispered Ehmet. "Wish me luck."

"Luck. Good luck. You know that." Milan disappeared around the corner.

If Ehmet could have become a part of the wall for the moment, he would have. In lieu of that, he clung to it and skittered in its shadow toward the back of the building and the warehouse. When he reached the back corner and the gate to the warehouse area, he stopped. Erik had left the gate open for the truck, same as yesterday. From where he was he could not see the truck or the men unloading it. Peeking around the corner to see what was happening could make him visible to them. He listened.

The driver's voice echoed with a metallic ring. Easy. He was in the back of the truck.

The two burly men were talkers. Ehmet could hear their voices clearly as they approached the truck, thumps as the driver dropped bags onto the truck bed for them to unload, and then their voices receding as they entered the warehouse.

Erik. Erik was the only one missing from the picture. Ehmet had to know where Erik was too before he could make his move. He didn't want Erik to have any possibility of seeing him. He strained to hear any telltale Erik noises.

The two burly men still gabbed, the driver called to them, and bags thudded through several rounds of carrying. Still no Erik. Then he heard a distant "Put them over here," through the babble of the two unloaders as they went into the warehouse. Erik was inside.

Ehmet made his move. He peeked around the corner and saw no one. The driver had parked the truck in the same position as yesterday. This was the picture Ehmet had been waiting for—the two unloaders and Erik inside the warehouse, the driver out of sight behind the walls of the truck box. From the angle Ehmet would be approaching, the driver could not see him, nor could the unloaders or Erik unless they came out of the building.

Ehmet streaked across open ground to the truck, hoping beyond hope that no one would suddenly appear. His heart pounded fiercely. He hoped he had it timed right, that the two men were just setting down their loads inside the warehouse with Erik directing.

Dodging into the shadows under the truck, Ehmet made himself as small as possible, crunched into a ball and tucked himself behind a pair of massive truck tires. From where he was he could not see the entry to the warehouse, and counted on the technique he had used for guidance before—I can't see them, they can't see me—working again. He waited apprehensively for a voice saying "Hey, what are you doing there?" Instead, the low-voiced rumbles of the two men coming back to the truck for another load were all that greeted him. The driver thumped a couple more sacks down onto the truck bed for the two to carry off: The sacks boomed on the floor of the truck as if they would crash right onto Ehmet.

The process of unloading cycled on in a regular rhythm. Ehmet kept himself tucked in the shadows, anticipating his next move, which was likely to be even more difficult than getting under the truck had been.

"That's all," said the driver finally.

The two made one more trip, voices receding into the warehouse, and returning loudly accompanied by Erik's. "Need anything more?" he asked the driver.

"Maybe just load the tarps and ropes back on while I do the paperwork."

Sounds of the crumpling cloth and coiled ropes that had secured the load hitting the bed of the truck mixed with the conversation of the two burly men.

"Thanks, you two," said Erik. "I'll meet you out front, then." One out, two to go.

After Erik left, Ehmet held his breath while he watched the feet of the driver pass on the way toward the truck cab.

The driver stopped, and a hand reached down to examine a truck tire within feet of Ehmet. If he bent any more he was certain to see him.

"Hey, nice truck." It was Milan's voice.

The hand pulled back from the tire. "Yeah, not a bad machine," said the driver continuing to walk toward the cab.

Good old Milan, thought Ehmet. Seeing what had been happening, that Ehmet might be spotted, he was trying to distract the driver.

Meanwhile above, the two men clumped around the truck floor, shuffling the tarps and ropes, then hopped down. Ehmet hoped they would head to the office and he could make his final move. No. Their feet passed the same way as the driver's, toward the front of the truck. They could not resist the opportunity to chat with the driver and find out what was happening in the outside world. The three laughed loudly at some joke.

This was it. Ehmet had to commit himself. Once the driver got out of the cab and closed the truck's back door, Ehmet would lose his chance. He inhaled, sucked in his stomach, held his backpack tight, and scurried to the tailgate of the truck. Easing himself onto the truck bed so as not to make noise, Ehmet could still hear the three talking. He padded to the pile of tarps and ropes, crawled under, and pulled the cloth over himself. It was dark.

◇

THIRTY-TWO

Light

There were as many stops going out as there were coming in. First stop was the front gate of the camp. Staying hidden under his protective cloth mountain, Ehmet felt that he would erupt like lava from the glowing heart of a volcano if he were exposed. No one opened the back of the truck.

Next stop was the roadblock where he had been searched on his way to the camp. He hoped they would not be interested in the emptied truck. He bounced along on the truck bed in anxious anticipation, dreading seeing the soldiers or their rumpled boss behind the desk.

When the truck rolled to a stop, Ehmet breathed shallowly, as if that would keep him from being heard, and closed his eyes, trying to maintain the darkness. If it stayed dark in his hideout, he had not been uncovered. He listened to the muffled voices outside discussing something, but he could not distinguish words. An age passed. Then he heard the creaks of the door being rolled open.

A hard point, maybe a gunbarrel, poked at the thick pile of

tarps and pressed against Ehmet's side. He tried to give, to make himself indistinguishable from the tarps, to become part of his cloth mountain. Ehmet opened his eyes.

All he saw was darkness. The pile still covered him. The soldiers were probably seeking cargo more valuable than what they saw as a pile of ragged packing materials. "Until next load, then," a voice that sounded like the nervous young soldier said as the rear door of the truck slammed closed.

Within minutes, the truck arrived in the town nearest the roadblock. The truck slowed, for traffic, Ehmet thought. He uncovered himself from his protective pile and slid to the back door. When the truck stopped, he eased the door open a crack just wide enough to slide under, and leaped.

He landed on the street in the light.

Ehmet blinked. The driver of the idling car he had landed in front of seemed mildly interested in Ehmet's appearance, but not shocked. Ehmet dodged by the car and paced up the sidewalk, away from the rear of the truck and the stalled traffic, keeping up his casual act. He did not turn around, so just his back would be visible should the truck driver look in his rearview mirror. Only when Ehmet heard the sounds of the truck and cars lurching into gear did he turn to look. The traffic signal had changed to green. The truck, followed by the cars, was pulling away from Ehmet.

Rounding the first corner he came to, out of sight of any people who might have seen him descend from the truck, Ehmet broke into a run. He ran, zigzagging, for blocks.

He turned another corner and slowed to a walk. Here he was again, a teenager walking the street of a town as if this was his life and his place and his time and he could once again decide. He passed a video shop with posters of superheroes, couples embracing, sweat-beaded men with guns, a dog show, aliens and space, various versions of worlds seen and unseen. Ehmet kept walking, laughed, working on his own version.

The warm, fragrant smell of a bakery hit him. He was drawn into the shop, bought several pastries that he devoured on the spot and a loaf of bread that he had wrapped in a bag to add it to his backpack for later. "Good?" asked the woman behind the counter.

"Very good," said Ehmet, wiping crumbs from around his mouth. Thinking that his ravenous consumption of the pastries might somehow unmask him, he added, "I love these lemon ones," as if it was an ordinary event for him to wolf down such quantities.

If she had noted his actions with any concern, the woman did not show it. She was pleased with the praise. "Here, have another, my treat."

"I'm pretty full," said Ehmet.

"That's all right. Take it, take it. I'll wrap it for later."

Ehmet thanked her and walked in the direction of the town square, where the long-distance buses arrived and departed. He stopped at a pay phone, took out his list, and made phone calls. He called his grandparents. Still no answers. He could head back to their house, but he was beginning to wonder if they would ever return there. Besides, that area was full of the soldiers and roadblocks that had gotten him into the camp. Having just escaped, he didn't want to risk that again.

The village Milan had told him about, where the Children's Village was, was located north toward the border with Italy. Milan had found it on Ehmet's map.

Ehmet asked the ticket seller for passage.

"No buses there from here. Practically no one lives up there. Closest you can get is this town." The ticket agent pointed to a dot on a map behind him. "It's not far from there, see?"

"A ticket there, then."

"One way?"

"One way."

Ehmet found an out-of-the-way nook, a bench under a spreading tree, and sat in dappled light that shifted patterns with the blowing branches, waiting for the bus.

THIRTY-THREE

Old Only

The town the ticket agent had directed Ehmet to popped into view practically before Ehmet registered he was traveling. This was his shortest ride yet—compressed in dense thought. Until now, Ehmet had been on roads that had not led him to those he hoped to find, though he had found Milan, and met Ali's family and Jakob and Danica. This time felt different.

He stepped off the bus into a town quieter than the one he had just left. The only person in sight was an old man sitting on a bench, leaning forward hunched on his cane with both hands folded over the handle for support. Ehmet asked him if there was a bus, how to get to the village.

"Walking. Used to be a bus, but hardly anyone lives there these days." The man spoke with an accent Ehmet did not recognize. "A lot of people moved away."

"Because of the war?"

"No. No war up here. Not this time, anyway," the old man said, staring into space and remembering other wars and other people.

"It's tough country for farmers. No work. Not enough work. A lot of people gone."

"Have you heard of some new people there, houses with a lot of kids?"

"Yes. I heard there are a few houses being fixed up. They come into town sometimes, buying supplies and such. You could wait for them."

"How often do they come into town?"

"A couple of times a week."

"I think I'll walk."

"Then take that road. You'll get there. Travel well."

"You, too."

The old man nodded.

At the edge of town, Ehmet came upon a rusting black-and-white metal sign with raised letters, pointing to the village. It indicated the village was nine miles away. Ehmet figured that three hours or less should do it. His legs were strong and solid, and he was ready to walk, even run. He did run the first mile, let the cool breeze slide by him with the countryside. He saw what the old man meant, that it was tough country for farming. It was hill country. The rocky hillsides topped by occasional villages rolled into the distance as far as Ehmet could see, and offered little flat terrain for fields.

Then he walked, winding with the road up hills, down, and up again. It was a single-lane, asphalt-paved road, patched but fairly smooth, perhaps in such good shape because not much vehicle traffic traveled on it. Not a car passed Ehmet. From time to time he would change his pace, naturally slowing uphill and flying down. Sky and the rolling, multi-colored hills, waves around Ehmet, were his own expansive ocean. He inhaled scents of damp earth and growing plants, heard new sounds, rustlings, stirrings, whistles, and calls.

Much of the land had returned to underbrush and trees, though evidence of a peopled past kept appearing—the hillsides' stepped terraces, some with remnants of the vineyards that had once covered them; ancient, wrist-thick grape vines twisting at the sun; olive and fruit trees still bearing fruit for animals that scurried beneath and flapped above.

Continuing along the road, ruins of ancient stone walls that had been fitted carefully stone by shaped stone were now woven with tree roots thrusting through and spotted with spiky plants and softer shapes of bushes that found footholds in the cracks of earth between fallen stones. In places, the flow of water had eroded small ravines in the walls, stones tumbled in heaps at the bases of miniature canyons.

Ehmet was immersed in the landscape as he climbed hill after hill. Ascending one more rise he was surprised to see stone walls newly maintained, holding terraces of neatly pruned vineyards and well-tended olive groves. A collection of stone houses, some with freshly stuccoed cement walls, most with old stonework still showing and red and orange clay-tile roofs, capped the hilltop. A medieval-looking, rectangular bell tower with a clock plumed the center.

Ehmet looked for people. The first stone house he came to at the edge of the village was closed, the windows covered by slatted, wooden shutters, green paint peeling from them. The second house looked inhabited, curtains and a potted plant with a handful of red blooms in the window, but he could not see anyone inside. Continuing the climb into the village, he passed more houses with shuttered windows like the first, and a number whose roofs and walls had caved in from untended exposure to years of weather. In another curtained house, an old woman held back a piece of material and peeked out. When she saw that Ehmet had spied her, she dodged into the dark interior and left the curtain fluttering.

In the walled-in backyard of the next house, a straight-bodied old man stood hoeing weeds out of his garden. He didn't pause when Ehmet approached.

"Excuse me. Can you tell me where the houses with a lot of kids are, the Children's Village?" The old man continued hoeing and gazed quizzically at Ehmet. "Mrs. Barisic, do you know Mrs. Barisic?"

Missing only half a beat in his hoeing rhythm, the old man pointed with his hoe at a building across the road and up a few houses.

"Thanks."

On a wall of the house the man had pointed out, Ehmet noticed patches of smooth, fresh cement, lighter gray than the surrounding weathered finish, and bright, new, orange clay roof tiles, repairs in the aged roof. A tall, handmade, wooden ladder leaned against another wall. Metal tools for working the cement were on the ground. It was a place under construction.

Ehmet knocked on the front door. A man he did not recognize answered. This could be the wrong place. Maybe the old man with the hoe had misunderstood him. "Can I help you?"

"Is . . . is Mrs. Barisic here?"

"No," said the man. Ehmet just stood there. "But she should be back soon. She is still at school." That made sense. If there was a school around, Mrs. Barisic was likely to be a part of it. "I'm her husband, Edin."

"Ehmet. I was one of her students. In Sarajevo."

"Come in, come in," said the man. "There's no reason for you to be standing in the street."

THIRTY-FOUR

◇

House and Home

Ehmet sat in the simple though comfortably furnished front room. "I would have invited you in anyway," said Edin. "That's what this house is, a place for kids, whether you were one of her students or not. How did you find out about us?"

"A friend."

"You've traveled far?"

"Not so far today," Ehmet said. He had become used to being protective about information.

"And otherwise?"

"Pretty far."

"Alone?"

"Mostly."

"You want to wait for Neda, eh? Here we call her Neda. She should be home soon." It was early evening. "Come with me. You can help us prepare dinner."

Ehmet picked up his backpack and started to follow Edin. "You can leave that," Edin said, referring to the backpack. "It'll be safe. That's one of the rules of the house, no stealing."

"That's all right," Ehmet said. He brought the pack along with him.

In the kitchen, two boys and a girl were busy washing and chopping vegetables. The girl, the oldest of the three, appeared to be a couple of years younger than Ehmet. The two boys were perhaps ten.

"This is Ehmet." Edin introduced him to the others. "This is Dejan." He had tousled hair and a serious look. "And Kemo." Kemo was neatly put together and moved with quick, nervous motions.

"Hey," said Kemo. Ehmet waved.

"And this is Sabrina." Ehmet found it difficult to tell much about her. She moved purposefully and her expression was somber and unchanging when he was introduced. He couldn't read her.

"Hello," she said, no more revealingly.

"Hello."

"So we all share in the work here," said Edin. Ehmet checked the reactions of the other kids. They looked agreeable. "Are you good at peeling?"

"Sure," said Ehmet.

Edin gave him a pile of potatoes, a pot, and a sharp-bladed vegetable peeler. "I'll be working in the next room, in the office, if you need me. I'll be back in a few minutes to help with the cooking."

Peeling the potatoes, Ehmet thought of the stories his grandfather told about how many potatoes he had peeled when he was in the army many years ago. His grandfather didn't talk about the battles, mostly just the potatoes.

"You're good at peeling potatoes," Sabrina said.

"An inherited skill," said Ehmet shortly, then softened. She was trying to talk to him. "What about you, what are you good at?"

"Peeling potatoes. Chopping onions. A few other things."

"I thought more than peeling potatoes. Have you been here long?"

"A couple of months." She kept washing lettuce leaves and neatly tearing them into bits.

"Are there other kids that live here?"

"A few."

"Do you know Mira?"

At that question the girl perked up. "Of course. You know Mira?"

"We went to school together."

"That's all?"

"That's all." Ehmet was not about to let her know more than that.

"She'll be here soon. She's with Neda at the school."

A chunk of red plinked against the outside of Ehmet's potato pot. It was a piece of a beet. Ehmet looked over at Kemo, who was chopping beets and smiling. "Hey," said Kemo.

"And what are you up to?" Ehmet tossed a piece of potato peel in Kemo's direction.

The flying food might have escalated, except for Mrs. Barisic and Mira appearing.

Mira leaned forward, peering in disbelief, and stumbled when she saw Ehmet. Then she hurried over and hugged him. Ehmet may have wanted, but was not ready for that. His blush approached beet color.

"Ehmet?" said Mrs. Barisic—Neda. He didn't know whether she was asking him because she hadn't seen him for a while and didn't recognize him, or because she was so surprised.

"Yes."

"How did you get here?" It was surprise.

"Walking mostly, buses."

"Alone?"

"Part of the way."

"It's good to see you," said Mira. She had taken a step back, and was standing between Ehmet and Sabrina.

"Good to see you," Ehmet responded, still a bit shaken. Now he registered that she had moved toward him unaided. "You are walking!"

"You mean with no crutches? I've got a new leg. Neda and Edin helped me get it." She reached down to below her knee and tapped with her knuckles. A hard, knocking sound echoed. "A little plastic and steel and I'm good as new. Almost. Maybe better. The bionic woman." She smiled. That was Mira. Couldn't stop her.

"He said you knew each other from school," said Sabrina.

"That's true," said Mira, looking at Ehmet for any signs.

"I can't believe you are here," said Neda. "Another person from the school."

Her husband, Edin, spoke up. Ehmet hadn't even noticed him come back into the kitchen with all the hoopla of Mira and Neda. "Ehmet just got here a short time ago. He wanted to talk to you."

"Let's have dinner first," said Neda. "Then we'll be more relaxed. I'm famished, and maybe Ehmet is, too. What do you think, Ehmet? We'll have plenty of time to talk."

"Yes," said Ehmet. Whether it was Neda's usual good sense, consideration for their all being tired, or that she had gotten an accurate read of how he was feeling, Ehmet was thankful not to launch into so much at the moment.

"I'm going to get cleaned up," said Mira, holding up multicolored, paint-covered hands.

"Good idea, Mary Cassatt. We were fixing up the school," Neda added, showing her own hands spattered with paint.

"You're part of the modern painting school," Ehmet said.

"Glad you haven't lost your sense of humor," said Neda. It was the kind of play on words she appreciated. Mira understood. The two boys and Sabrina looked at him as if he were from another planet. Maybe he was.

THIRTY-FIVE

Dinner

At dinner, Ehmet met the additional four children in the house, two boys and two girls younger than Ehmet and Mira. Dinner was like a family affair around a large table. That was the idea, Neda told him, that this was their family. Most of the conversation centered on events of the day, of the present, projects in which each of them and the group were involved, rebuilding the house and school, restoring terrace walls and gardens. And the kinds of stories that might be heard at a family dinner anywhere—about the toad Dejan brought to school that escaped to squeals and leaping in the classroom; about the mural of the galaxy Sabrina was drawing in her room with swirls of stars and planets.

From what Milan had told him at the camp, Ehmet knew how Mira had come to be here. Details about the other kids' pasts did not come out much, though some referred to this place or that. They came from all over Bosnia, Croatia, and Serbia. Ehmet told them briefly that he'd left Sarajevo, a little about getting here, and that he hoped to find his father, his grandparents, and some of his other relatives. He skipped the part about his mother for the moment; he didn't want to get into that.

He mentioned the silent old man with the hoe who had finally directed him to the house. Ehmet was curious about him.

"Oh yes, that's Antonio. He's a very nice neighbor," said Neda.

"He didn't talk with me."

"Do you speak Italian?"

"No."

"The older people around here mostly speak Italian. For a long time, until the Second War, this was Italy. Everyone in the house is trying to learn Italian."

"Yes," added Edin, "that's another project."

That explained why the dinner conversation was peppered with Italian words.

"*Grazie,*" Mira said when Ehmet handed a bowl to her across the table. "*Per favore, lo mandi a cuesto indirizzo.*"

Neda and Edin and a couple of kids laughed. Kemo said to Ehmet, "She just said, 'Please send it to this address.' We learned that today."

"It's what I meant to say," Mira said.

After dinner, everyone carried plates and dinnerware into the kitchen. Ehmet and Mira managed to stroll in together, their first opportunity to talk almost in private. Mira's steps were uneven, she was still getting used to the differences in her legs, but she was walking. They ran into no resistance when they volunteered to wash the dishes so they could stand together at the sink. They splashed water on each other and laughed and talked, though not about anything important since there were a lot of listening ears nearby.

"Let's go for a walk," Mira whispered to Ehmet when they had nearly exhausted the supply of things to wash.

"Okay," said Ehmet. He didn't need a lot of convincing. "Where?"

"Around the village. It'll be fine. I'll ask."

It had been a long time since Ehmet had been able to take a walk in the evening without having to worry about what might happen. In Sarajevo, there had been the shelling and snipers.

On his journey here, every step had been a wary one. The idea of taking a walk for pleasure felt novel.

Neda and Edin were hesitant to let them go, though. "I thought Ehmet and I were going to talk," said Neda. "Ehmet?"

"We can talk after Mira and I get back."

"Besides, I'm not exactly a long-distance runner with this yet," said Mira, tapping her leg. "It'll be good practice."

"Yes, the more practice, the better. Okay. Edin and I have some things to talk about anyway." Edin nodded. "Ehmet, when you get back," Neda confirmed.

The village was amazingly quiet. When Ehmet and Mira weren't talking, their feet softly thudding on the cobblestone streets were the only sounds.

"It's like there's nobody living here," said Ehmet.

"There aren't that many people," Mira said. "Before Neda and Edin and their friends started bringing kids and fixing up houses, there were sixty people in the whole village. I've started to get to know some. There were mostly older people, no families with little kids. They'd all moved away to find work. There wasn't even much of a school anymore, that's why we've been fixing it up. It's really different for them having kids around. We're too noisy for a few of them."

"It's easy to be noisy where there is no other noise."

"They're just not used to it. And some people are worried about what we're really like or what we'll do to their village. You can tell from the way they look at us. They haven't been dealing with a lot of outsiders. I just try to smile back." Mira turned and demonstrated for Ehmet. He thought about reaching out to touch her face.

She pointed at a house diagonally across the street. "That's another house that's part of the group, with kids. There are three houses so far."

"How many kids?"

"Twenty-four total right now. Twenty-five with you. I think the plan is for maybe forty. You'll never guess who lives in that house." She pointed again.

"I have no clue."

"Someone you know from our school in Sarajevo."

"Who?"

"Who would you least like to see?"

"Darko."

"Right, Darko."

"Darko!" Ehmet called out his name loudly in shock.

"Now that's noisy," Mira chuckled.

"Darko." Ehmet shook his head.

"I told you, you wouldn't believe it. He's changed a little."

"That's even harder to believe."

"Something happened to him. I don't know what it was, he won't talk about it. But it was something big."

"Must have been," said Ehmet, "bigger than Darko. When Neda said there was someone else from the school here, I thought she meant you."

"Don't worry about Darko. That's why I didn't tell you before. Probably why Neda didn't either. Didn't want to alarm you. The people, I mean besides her, her friends, too, they really try to help. I'm glad I'm here. I mean, I wish I hadn't had to be, but it's good."

They walked on in silence. Ehmet reached for Mira's hand. She held his evenly, squeezed his fingers.

"Can we sit down?" Mira suggested. They were next to a low, flat-topped, stone wall that would make a decent bench.

"Good by me," said Ehmet.

From their perch on the wall they looked out from the hilltop village, across silhouette hills to small clumps of glistening lights in distant villages. A few light clouds wisped past vast spatters of stars. "The sky is so clear here," said Mira. She tipped her head up and blew white streams of condensed breath into the dark sky. Ehmet tried to blow one of his own breaths into a circle. The two sent a series of small clouds in bursts into the cold autumn air. Tonight Ehmet hadn't noticed the cold until now. The two of them tucked themselves to sit tight together.

"I have dreams again," said Mira. Ehmet wasn't sure what she meant. "Lately, I want to be a doctor or a journalist."

"A doctor or a journalist?"

"Oh yes, a doctor so I can cure your ills, or a journalist so I can tell the news when it happens," Mira teased. "Really. I'd like to try to help people."

"A journalist. You want to try to help people? My father's a journalist. He thinks if people just know what's going on, they'll do the right thing."

"If they don't know, how can they make decisions?"

"A lot of good that's been doing."

"You're really angry at him?"

"He sent my mother and me off. My mother died!"

"Where did he send you?"

"To the countryside. My aunt and uncle's."

"He thought you'd be safe there?"

"Yes."

"What about your mom?"

"She thought so, too. But we weren't."

"So was that your father's fault?"

"He should have been with us."

Mira sat thinking. "My father was next to me when he died. I know he wanted to protect me, but he couldn't, no matter where he was. A shell blew up, he was gone. And my leg, before either of us had a chance to do anything. I've thought, 'Why did it happen? What could I have done?' I don't think there are answers to some questions. Do you think it was my fault?"

"Of course not!" said Ehmet.

"Same with your father. I don't think it was his fault. He was probably doing the best he knew how to try to protect you. Maybe by trying to make the world safer or saner, too. How about not having these guys shooting at us? What else could we do except try against the craziness? Do you think it was your fault, what happened to your mother?"

Mira had put into words what Ehmet had been haunted by ever since that night at the farm and in their journey, that he should have done something other than what he did, that he should have protected her. He turned away from Mira and tears soaked his face. She waited for him to speak. When he did he told her about the farm, about the journey together and his alone, about seeing Milan and the camp and leaving it.

"And you think it might have been your fault? Starting with the farm? A truckload of guys with guns? Your uncle was there, and your aunt, and they couldn't stop it. You did what your mother and you had agreed, what she had asked you to do. Then you thought she had a cold, and that's what she told you, too. It's not your fault, it's not her fault. Anyone can say they should have known what to do, done something else, after something's happened. You think you're Superman with X-ray vision?"

"No on the Superman. And a little blurry, the X-ray vision." He was shaking, whether from the cold or the conversation he wasn't sure.

"Come on," said Mira, "I've been thinking about this stuff for months. And we both will be for a lot longer than that. Let's go back to the house, where it's warm."

Ehmet was confused. One of the people he admired most had just told him she believed in what one of the people he was most angry at, his father, was doing. Mira was one of the people he felt closest to and she could be a pain, all at the same time. No, she wasn't really the pain.

At the house, Neda and Edin were waiting in the front room. "That was a long walk," said Neda.

"It was beautiful out there," said Mira. "And we were talking."

"That's good," said Edin.

"Can we talk now?" Neda asked Ehmet.

"I guess so," said Ehmet. A lot of new thoughts were kicking around in his head. His confusion was palpable, but so was his desire to try to straighten things out. Better now than in the morning. The kind of conversation he was going to have, he didn't want to have in front of the other kids, whom he didn't know. They were already asleep upstairs.

"I'm going to go to sleep now, too," Mira said. "See you in the morning, Ehmet."

"See you." Mira disappeared up the stairs.

"Would you like me to leave?" Edin asked.

"No, that's okay," Ehmet said. He had gotten to know Edin a bit at dinner, and felt comfortable with him. Also, Edin and Neda seemed to work well as parts of a team.

"Good," said Neda. "The main thing we want you to know is that we will do anything we can to help you."

"I know." Ehmet expanded on what he had mentioned at dinner about leaving Sarajevo and his father, his searches for his family, and told them about his mother's death on the journey.

"I'm sorry to hear about your mother," said Neda. "I knew her, because of you at school, and really liked her, too. A wonderful person. As far as looking for the rest of your family, I'm hoping we can help there," said Neda.

"We have a lot of contacts," Edin added.

"Yes. We'll use whatever information you can give us, and we know people who work with many agencies, work with refugee groups, health organizations, that can help locate people. It's kind of detective work. We'll get some clues, and track them."

"We can start tonight," said Edin.

Ehmet copied his list of phone numbers and addresses for them in the room they used as an office. Edin immediately clattered at a keyboard, entering more information into a computer.

After Neda showed Ehmet to an empty bedroom down the hall and he stashed his pack by the bed, he could hear her back in the office making telephone calls, mentioning names he recognized. With those humming in his ears, he fell asleep.

THIRTY-SIX

Finders Keepers

The days that followed were full of surprises for Ehmet. Even when he thought he knew what to expect, unexpected pieces kept dropping in.

First, there was Darko. Ehmet encountered him the day after arriving. It was Saturday, and all three households of kids and adults were involved in a project—rebuilding a stone wall to hold a terraced garden for growing vegetables. The day was crisp and cold, the sky bright blue, the sun brilliant except when Darko's big frame blocked it out.

Ehmet had tried to stay away from him as Mira had suggested. But part of the idea of these group projects was for everyone to get to know each other better, to interact, and the nature of what they were doing: handing loose stones to each other in a line, others working together to fit and place the stones into the wall, brought a changing cast of people to everyone's side. Ehmet and Mira had been working together in the warm, midmorning light. People on the terrace above would carry loose stones and hand them down to Mira and Ehmet, who would place them in the wall. They were both enjoying the sight of the piled stones being formed by their work into something useful and, they thought, attractive.

"Yup, another sculptural masterpiece," said Mira jokingly.

Small stones Ehmet and Mira each handled individually, larger stones they reached up and brought down together. All went well until a shadow fell over the two of them. At first, Ehmet did not recognize whose the shadow was. He simply saw a dark silhouette standing above, the bright light that shined from behind the figure blinding Ehmet to any distinct features. Only when he squinted did he determine that it was Darko holding a large stone, what could be called a boulder.

"It's a big one, they asked me to carry it to you," Darko said. That was old Darko, bragging, thought Ehmet. Yet from his tone, it was as if Darko was apologetic for disturbing them. Ehmet might have believed that, except for what happened next.

Darko squatted to hand the boulder to Ehmet and Mira. Both reached up to grasp it, but before they had a firm grip the stone dropped from Darko's hands, thundering toward Mira and Ehmet. Ehmet tried to cling to the stone and pull it toward him. As the boulder fell, more freefall than a controlled drop, his left hand was smashed between it and a rock in the wall.

Ehmet cradled the gashed left hand in his right. It was numb and throbbing with blood. He looked at Darko, who was standing on the terrace above with his mouth hanging open. Without thinking, Ehmet leaped onto the terrace. He shot upward with a warehouse full of built-up anger at Darko, at all the people who had gashed and mashed his and his family's lives.

Before Darko reacted—he was still standing with his mouth open—Ehmet jammed his hands against Darko's chest, heaving the big boy backward over the edge of the terrace. Darko tumbled onto the earth below. Ehmet stepped to the edge and peered down. To his surprise, Darko did not have the fierce look Ehmet had seen so many times from him. He appeared to be shocked. Ehmet looked to Mira, still sitting a few feet from where Darko lay in a heap. Ehmet realized now he could have hurt her, too, when he pushed Darko off the edge. Darko might have fallen on her. Ehmet jumped down to see how she was doing.

"Ehmet. Ehmet!" Edin and Neda shouted. They had seen Darko's fall and thought Ehmet was leaping at him again. They arrived at a panting run to find Ehmet sitting by Mira, and Darko pulling himself to his feet. Darko's chest was covered with blood. Edin and Neda gaped at his bloody chest.

"It's his," said Darko. "Blood from Ehmet's hand," sweeping his own hand against the blood, trying to rub it off himself.

"My hand," Ehmet said, holding it up. "He dropped that rock on us."

"I'm fine," said Mira. "Nothing and nobody fell on me."

"It was an accident," said Darko.

"Right," Ehmet said.

"That's it, you two. No physical fights. Darko, you know that. You too, Ehmet," Edin said.

"They have a history," said Neda.

"I know," said Edin. "Everyone here has a history. If everyone with a history fights, we're in big trouble. Darko, you know how this goes. Find a spot to sit and think for a while, until you and Ehmet can talk. You will have to work things out."

"Ehmet, let's take care of your hand first," Neda said.

She rinsed Ehmet's hand with water from a bottle. The gash was bloody, though not that deep. A patch of tape that Neda pulled from her pocket took care of it. She kept things in a "we need that" way.

"I can still work," said Ehmet. He didn't want to be left out of the activity, especially working with Mira.

"You need to work things out with Darko. Sit and think about what you want to say."

Ehmet sat on the edge of a wall watching the group work. The walls to support the earthen garden terraces were taking shape stone by stone. Mira glanced over at him from time to time, but she was working too far away to talk. Darko sat at the far end of the field.

After an hour or so, with neither Ehmet nor Darko having made a move, Edin checked in with Ehmet.

"Are you ready?"

"To go back to work?"

"To talk to Darko."

"I really don't want to talk with him."

"Hmm. He said the same thing. We can't risk having the two of you blow up like mines. Dangerous for you and the people around you. There's no other way. Unless you want to try to work together, just the two of you. If you can show that you've worked things out, then you can come back and work with everyone."

Ehmet weighed the prospects. Big Darko kept tipping the scale, but the pull of Mira and the rest of the group was greater. "I can do it."

"I'll ask Darko, see if he wants to do the same." Edin trotted over to where Darko was sitting and spoke to him. He motioned Ehmet to join the two of them.

"He says he can do it, too," Edin said.

"Yeah," Darko said.

"Alright then. For now, you two work on your own. The two of you can partner and move those loose stones over to that pile. We'll use them to build with later." Hearing the word 'partner' in reference to Darko was almost enough to make Ehmet physically sick. He thought about walking away, but that would end the deal and Ehmet would be back to sitting.

"Ready, Darko?"

"Sure thing."

Edin went back to working with the group, yet kept an eye on the two of them.

At first it was easy. Each of them found stones small and light enough to carry individually. There were plenty of those spread across their end of the field, so each found stones as far as he could from the other and carried them to the growing pile. They kept out of each other's way, working at the far edges of the field. Little by little though, the supply of small distant stones was exhausted, and they found themselves working in a circle that constantly diminished in size.

Ehmet spotted a stone and started toward it.

"I'll take that one," said Darko.

"That one's mine," Ehmet insisted.

"Suit yourself. It's a big one." Darko shrugged and ambled off.

Ehmet studied the stone. Then he laughed at himself. He had been ready to fight over a rock. It would take the two of them to carry it.

"Maybe together," suggested Ehmet. Darko walked over and picked up one side, and Ehmet took the other. The stone slid unevenly between Darko's tall frame and Ehmet's more compact one. With a bit of adjustment they managed to balance it between them. Walking was another trick; they had to synchronize their gaits so as not to stumble. Ehmet realized they probably presented a comical picture as they zigzagged across the field. They grunted from the effort, but broke into laughter as the weight of a stone took over, swinging them from here to there.

Other stones were easier, and finally they heaved the last from their section of the field onto the heap. Ehmet climbed to the top and collapsed. Darko joined him. They sat on their lumpy pyramid and surveyed the landscape.

"Nice work," said Ehmet.

"Oh yeah. You know, it really was an accident."

"Us piling up these stones?"

"Me dropping that rock. I lost my grip. I wouldn't have wanted to hurt Mira." Darko added sheepishly, "I like her."

"I thought you hated her. The things you used to try to do to her in school . . ."

"I don't know. About then. I wanted her to notice me, anyway."

Ehmet started to get a different picture.

"We're not best buddies," said Darko. "I still feel like kicking your butt. I'm pissed off. Maybe not at you. I'm tired of fighting. With you, with anybody. Your blood." He pointed to the splotches he had not been able to clean from his chest. "I hate seeing blood. Seen more than anyone should see. *Boom*, no family."

Ehmet turned to look at Darko. "How did you get here?"

"Mrs. Barisic found me. On a list she got of kids who needed homes. She saw my name, and asked if they could bring me here. I can't believe she did that, after all the things I did in her class."

"She likes kids."

"Lucky she does. The others here, too. In the prison camp they didn't care whether I was a kid or not."

"Prison camp?"

"I joined up to fight for the Croat militia. I was big, they took me." He looked at Ehmet. "They probably would have taken you, too."

"But I'm not pure Croat, remember. You used to tell me that."

"Anyway, my dad and I both joined. Within a week of fighting, my dad was . . . dead. And I was in a Serb prison camp. Lucky I got exchanged when the Croat and Serb big shots traded prisoners. The guys who stayed in the camp . . . "

"Stinks."

"Yeah. My mom's gone, too. You're still looking for some people?"

"My dad. My grandparents. I don't know."

"Yeah."

Edin approached them. "It looks like you two have figured some things out. Ready to come back with the rest of us?" Both nodded yes.

Ehmet sidled back to Mira to help finish stacking stones on top of a wall. "He says it was an accident."

"You believe him?"

"Not sure."

"How's your hand?"

"Fine. You okay?"

"Absolutely. What a mess that was. At least you and Darko didn't throw the stones at each other. I'm glad you found a way to get back here."

THIRTY-SEVEN

Change

The weeks following Ehmet's arrival were full of changes, and of things staying the same.

Ehmet still couldn't find his family.

He watched new families being formed around him, with the many changes that required. Kids had to accept new adults as parents, new kids as brothers and sisters. Both the kids and adults had a huge range of experiences and backgrounds—Bosnian, Croat, Serb, Christian, Jewish, Muslim—and a lot to learn about one another. But overall, the lives they were creating in this village could handle the inevitable curveball.

Ehmet went to the local school—which was made up mostly of kids from the Children's Village who had helped rebuild it, and tried to catch up with what the class had been studying this year. After school, kids from the village and surrounding farms dribbled a basketball around the asphalt court next to the school building. Basketball was big here. Some of the kids had moves, could weave with the ball down the court as if no one was in the way. A few had basketball dreams. Croatians, Serbs, and

Bosnians, too, had recently made teams in the U.S., Canada, Europe—all over the world.

Yet it was soccer that Ehmet really wanted to play. The locals had a soccer team. Some weekday evenings and practically every Sunday afternoon, there were matches with teams from neighboring villages, towns, and even farther away. The thing was, everyone had a uniform and a position. Since no one was sure Ehmet would be in the village for very long, they were hesitant to have him take a place on the team and give him a uniform. The first few games, Ehmet stood on the sidelines, cheering with Mira.

Ehmet couldn't give up the idea of playing soccer, in whatever form. He set up a makeshift goal with cans to mark the corners on a grassy patch next to the basketball court and would dribble around with anyone else who wanted to play. A few of the teens and young men on the village team stopped to watch as Ehmet glided across his field and slapped the soccer ball into the goal.

One afternoon the coach of the local team, who also played on it—the best player, in his late twenties—walked up to Ehmet. "Want to join the team?"

"Absolutely," said Ehmet.

He bubbled with enthusiasm as he told Mira, then realized how she might feel.

She caught him glancing down, and slapped her leg. "Don't worry, I'd probably kick their butts. There are no girls on the team anyway."

Ehmet joined the practices, and got a jersey with a number—three.

Mira continued to watch from the sidelines during games . . . and so did Ehmet. He couldn't understand why he wasn't put in to play more—he thought he'd been playing well. He was quick, faster than he'd ever been, could get by Darko easily in practices.

After a couple of weeks, he asked the coach why he wasn't playing in the games much.

"You're good. I can't risk the team getting too used to relying on you. We don't know how long you'll be in the village—when you'll find your family," the coach reminded him.

Ehmet was in limbo. He helped around the house and village. In the hubbub of the evenings, with nine kids trying to do home-work or practicing musical instruments, Neda and Edin were kept in an endless cycle of emergency answering: "Neda, can you look at this story?" "Listen to this." "Edin, I don't understand the math." Ehmet was a much-sought-after tutor. At those times, he felt a part of the place.

"We found him!" Neda ran to tell Ehmet one day. "Actually he found us! I just got a call. Come in here." She handed him the phone.

"Ehmet!" Through a crackling connection, Ehmet heard what sounded like his father's voice.

"Dad?"

"You're . . . all right?" he thought his father asked. But the con-nection was so bad, he wasn't sure.

"Yes." Ehmet answered.

"Can't . . . hear." The connection crackled. "See you . . . tomor-row." Ehmet thought his father said.

"Tomorrow?" Ehmet asked as the line went dead.

After Ehmet got off the phone he was excited, and uneasy. The world was about to change again, and he was not sure how.

THIRTY-EIGHT

◇

The Village

In the morning Ehmet popped awake, wondering. He ate breakfast without saying much, and went to school. Edin and Neda had offered to have him stay at the house with one of them, but he wanted to keep busy, be a part of the routines he had become accustomed to and see the kids he'd been getting to know.

Darko cornered Ehmet after lunch. He had heard. "You're lucky," Darko said.

When Ehmet managed to get a minute with Mira, and she saw his uneasiness, she was clear. "It's great that you're getting family back. We'll work it out."

After school, as Ehmet waited, Neda and Edin explained how his father had found him.

When Neda and Edin had given the names of his family to their contacts and no one could locate them, the two of them had asked that if any of his family showed up, to get in touch. Neda told him that someone from the Red Cross had helped place the call here yesterday.

His grandparents had been looking for Ehmet, his mother,

aunt, and uncle, as well as his father. That was why Ehmet hadn't been able to get ahold of them, they had been traveling all over Croatia and as far as they could get into Bosnia, trying to find the family. It was his Aunt Boda and then his father they had found first. They were continuing to look for the rest of the family.

"It hasn't been easy, and your father got out of the camp only days ago," Neda said. "We want you to be ready, at least for the way he might look."

Ehmet squirmed.

"Everyone will have adjusting to do," Edin said. "What do you think?"

"I'm glad, I guess, he's getting here. But I'm not sure about leaving."

A knock on the door ended the conversation.

Ehmet answered.

The first thing that fell away was his anger. He hadn't realized how tightly he had held it until it started disappearing. His father was a toothpick. He couldn't be angry at a toothpick. Just a thin coating of flesh and skin was holding together the skeleton of the man he had known before.

His father saw the look of shock on Ehmet's face. "Don't worry, a little food, and I'll be back in business." He reached to wrap his arms around Ehmet.

Ehmet could feel his father's bones angling through. He put out his own arms, and was sure they could wrap around his father a couple of times. He was afraid to press too hard, his father looked so fragile.

"I won't break," his father said. "Been tried. Great to see you," he said. "Great." He held on to Ehmet.

They found themselves standing in the doorway. Neda and Edin welcomed his father and invited him into the house. They spoke with him briefly, then left the two to talk on their own.

Ehmet's father had been taken prisoner by a plainclothes armed gang who said they were Serb militia. It was when he was on his way to see for himself what was happening in Sarajevo's Old City, which had been heavily shelled. He had planned to write about it.

"They found that dangerous," his father said. "Information was a weapon they wanted to control." He had been put in what they called a prison, though was simply a decrepit warehouse. One cold drafty room with no bathroom, where two hundred "prisoners" slept on the damp, cement floor, and were starved and regularly beaten, some were whisked away and never seen again. It was from that place that Ehmet's grandparents had gotten Ehmet's father released.

Ehmet's grandfather and grandmother had searched refugee camps, checked with offices, and contacted every local and international help organization they could until they found Ehmet's Aunt Boda. She had told them something of what had happened at the farm that night. They had continued to search for Ehmet and his mother and Uncle Petar—so far without finding him—and for Ehmet's father. In their searches, they heard about "secret" prison camps not open to anyone or any organization, some run by Serbs, others by Croats. The only information they had about Ehmet's father was what Ehmet had also found, that he had last been heard from going to the Old City. Ehmet's grandfather, suspecting, hoping that his father, Petar, and Ehmet and his mother had not been killed but taken prisoner and were still alive, had called on every old army connection he knew, and more, to try and find them.

At first, even his grandfather's friends had denied that secret camps existed. But his grandparents had persisted, and on the third visit to one of his grandfather's old friends, the man had said he "might know someone who knew someone, who knew about the prison camps." During the weeks Ehmet had been trying to locate his grandparents they had been going from person to person, place to place, searching for him and the rest of the family. Several days ago they had gotten word that Ehmet's father had been located.

Ehmet's grandfather had called in several favors, one a life he had saved years ago, to arrange for Ehmet's father's release into the hands of Doctors Without Borders for medical treatment. While his grandmother had stayed with Aunt Boda to nurse her back to health near the camp where she had been held, his grandfather confirmed Ehmet's father's release and hurried on to try to find Uncle Petar, who he had just heard was rumored to have been seen shortly after his capture, under guard digging ditches in a village near the farmhouse. Ehmet and his mother had remained unaccounted for.

Immediately upon his own release, Ehmet's father had phoned and searched every list and keeper of lists he could get ahold of for Ehmet and his mother. The detective skills he had honed as a journalist had uncovered Ehmet's being here.

Ehmet tried to catch him up on what had occurred on his journey. He told him most about his mother. His father was full of questions, which he answered. Ehmet's father held his own face in his hands and shook his head from side to side. "I should have . . . I don't know. I spent every penny we had to get you two out of Sarajevo. I thought you and your mother would be safe there . . . " The two of them swam wordlessly through drifting thoughts.

Ehmet broke out. "I tried to do what I could . . . "

"Sounds like pneumonia," said his father. "It can happen in a day. There is no way you could have known, she probably didn't either except that she felt bad. Nothing more you could have done without medical help. Or maybe with anyone's . . . my help." They sat quietly together, and cried.

Ehmet felt he'd had enough sadness for several lifetimes. What he'd been discovering in this village had begun to make life seem good again. Ehmet tried to describe his new life. His father listened. His grim expression appeared to warm.

Neda and Edin returned and invited his father for dinner and to spend the night. He had had a long day getting here. In the morning, he could begin afresh.

At dinner, Ehmet's father met all of the family of the house.

"Dad, remember Mira?"

His father nodded and searched Ehmet's eyes. "Good seeing you, Mira."

After dinner, Ehmet suggested to Mira they take a walk. He was not sure when he would be able to do that again. He looked at his father.

"Certainly," said his father. "Besides, I'd like to talk with Neda and Edin." It turned out his father had known both of them better than Ehmet had suspected in Sarajevo. He felt even closer to them after what they had done for Ehmet. The three of them were talking in the front room when Ehmet and Mira went out.

Their walk was as beautiful as on any night. The two of them spoke little. Both the uncertainties of what might happen between them and the difficulty of putting so much into words, left them in a full, rich silence.

"We've got to keep in touch," Ehmet said at last.

"I promise," said Mira.

When they returned to the house, Neda, Edin, and Ehmet's father were still seated, talking. "Come on in," Ehmet's father invited. He was beaming. Somewhere in the conversation he had found hope, thought Ehmet.

Mira started toward the stairs, uncertain of where she might fit in this scenario. "Mira, Mira, it's fine. We're just going to talk a bit. You are welcome," Ehmet's father said. Mira and Ehmet found chairs. What his father suggested in the conversation following shocked Ehmet as much as their earlier conversations, in a very different way.

"You've inspired me," Ehmet's father said to him. "You've done it before, though you may not have known it. In the camp, thinking about you and your mother, what I would like to do, was almost all I thought about." He paused. Ehmet answered only with a stare. There was a lot to work out.

His father continued. "What is happening in this village, what you've all been doing . . . we can't easily go back to Sarajevo right now . . . I need to recuperate, and I can write anywhere, about anything. It's a portable profession. There's a world to write about here. You and me have a pile of things to figure out. Your grandparents, they're still helping Boda get on her feet and searching for Petar. We can see them soon. Besides, they'll only be a couple of hours away. We can visit them easily, or they us. Neda and Edin have told me there are any number of buildings here you and I could live in and fix up. They are thinking of adding one more household to the group . . . maybe . . . what do you think?"

It had been such a mountainous talk from his father that Ehmet had hardly been able to register all of it. Yet it penetrated. From deep within he laughed, a thunderous, village-rocking laugh.

AUTHOR'S NOTE

◇

In June 1991, the southeast European country of Yugoslavia began to split apart. Slovenia, one of the six republics that made up Yugoslavia, declared and gained its independence after brief fighting. The republic of Croatia also opted for independence, which brought it into prolonged conflict with the Yugoslav national army, the Serb republic, and militias. Macedonia, another republic, soon chose to become a separate state as well. The republic of Bosnia and Herzegovina (commonly called simply Bosnia), was the most ethnically and religiously diverse of the former Yugoslav republics, with large groups of citizens who could identify themselves as Croat, Serb, Muslim, of mixed backgrounds, or as being from other, smaller, groups. When Bosnia declared its own independence in March 1992, the announcement was followed by intense fighting—backed by neighboring republics—among groups that had lived side-by-side for hundreds of years. The war in Bosnia lasted for almost four years, officially ending with what were called the Dayton Peace Accords. Peace is still taking shape.

This is a story of surprise and light, though it didn't start that way. For years I heard, read, and saw news of the wars in the region. These conflicts were frequently portrayed as struggles between ethnic groups. Then friends told me of an ancient village in Croatia that was being rebuilt by a mixed group of people from the backgrounds most often named in the conflicts—Croat, Serb, and Muslim. The group was composed of children many of whom were orphans or refugees from the fighting, and a few adults. I read about and saw photographs of the place. In this picturesque medieval hilltop village that had been largely abandoned in past decades, walls were being refitted stone by stone, cement resmoothed, red tile roofs patched. Families were being re-formed, lives sprouting and growing as potently as the newly planted gardens around them. I did not know if such a place truly existed, but if it did, I could imagine a survivor of war torn lands wending his or her way toward it.

Before I visited, I wondered if the village was really as great as it sounded. Maybe the "warts" had been erased from the pretty picture. I was surprised to find that it was even better than described. This peaceful place had been built with the imaginations and efforts of four hardworking, warm families, each composed of about ten children and foster children with an adult couple dedicated to being mother and father, healers and providers of home.

This story is not meant to depict that place and people, but it was inspired by them. It is the story of a boy making his way through war to a place of hope. As I wrote it, I read news articles, histories, and memoirs, and talked with people who had lived through these and other conflicts. I remembered my own family's stories of making ways through the war-shredded Eastern Europe of an earlier time—hiding in hay wagons, skating by border guards—in order to awake in places where life and hope could thrive. One of my grandfathers crossed a border by popping on a baseball cap, smoking a cigar, leaping from a train—and found himself in a new land.

I did not set out to nor could I possibly explain the complex history of the region. Anyway, as with all history, the answer to who did what can easily be different depending on the person telling. But because this story includes events that some might recognize and others not, I will give a little more background.

In a land just across the beautiful Adriatic Sea and neighbor to Italy, are countries that in the past few years have been known as Croatia, Bosnia and Herzegovina ("Bosnia"), the Federal Republic of Yugoslavia (consisting of Serbia and Montenegro),

Macedonia, and Slovenia. These new countries had been parts of what was for decades the single country of Yugoslavia.

In the thousands of years before, different peoples—Venetians, Italians, Austrians, Turks, and others—held these lands. After World War II, the region became six republics united under the umbrella of Yugoslavia, with a Communist government headed by Josip Broz, "Tito." Tito had risen to power resisting the Nazis in World War II; he then held Yugoslavia in his political grip until he died in 1980. After Tito, and with the deterioration of Communism, some of the republics started attempting to separate. In these republics lived a mix of peoples who identified themselves with an array of ethnic and religious backgrounds, including Serb, Croat, Muslim, Jewish, and Roma (Gypsy). The Croats tended to be Catholic; Serbs were typically Serbian Orthodox—another, related, form of Christianity. However, there were, for instance, Muslims, Jews, and Roma living in Serbia and Croatia. Some of these populations were severely diminished during World War II, but people of the various backgrounds remained spread throughout the republics.

These peoples did not, as a whole, look physically different one from another. It was often a person's name that indicated his or her roots. For example, Alija is a Muslim name; Ivan likely Croat; Zoran, Serb; the same with particular surnames. But in Bosnia in particular, a person's name couldn't tell the whole story.

Before the wars of the 1990s, the population of Bosnia was the most mixed. In a total population of around four and a half million, close to two million people identified themselves as having Muslim roots, dating from the time the Ottoman Turks controlled the region. There were nearly as many Bosnian Serbs—a million and a half—and three-quarters of a million Croats, with smaller numbers of Roma, Jews, and people of other backgrounds. The capital of Bosnia, Sarajevo, was known as a place where people of different backgrounds had lived together as neighbors for hundreds of years, and, in fact, often as parts of the same families. At the start of the war there were almost no neighborhoods in Sarajevo identified with any specific ethni group, and in Bosnia and Herzegovina overall, as many as forty percent of all families were made up of people of two or more backgrounds.

So when I visited Bosnia, I had another surprise. Unlike what the news reports had led me to believe, these lands were not full of people brimming with ethnic or religious hatred. Almost everyone I met told me the same thing: It was not so much ethnic divisions that drove the conflicts as economics and grabs for power. Certainly there is a history of ethnic animosities in the region, and this history was drawn on to fuel the conflicts by those seeking power or economic gain. A saying I heard and paraphrase here summarizes the view I often encountered:

> *The poor send their sons to war.*
> *The rich send money.*
> *Those in power profit.*

The fact that these conflicts were not necessarily driven by ethnic differences in the region should not have been surprising. To separate ethnic groups in Bosnia would be to separate husbands and wives, fathers and mothers, sisters and brothers, or parts of one's self. What part would be Serb or Croat, Jewish or Muslim? Many families were ripped apart.

Some of the children and adults at the real "Children's Village," Nadomak Sunca, in Oprtalj, Croatia, came from such situations; and continue to demonstrate ways to put the pieces back together with joy. Not long ago, I saw artwork by a few of these kids; phenomenal, bright drawings that show just some of the skills and spirit they continue to grow. A caption on a drawing of one of the new homes read: "This house is for me a golden sun. I am telling you the living truth, the truth that comes from my heart."

ACKNOWLEDGMENTS

When I have seen acknowledgments in books before, I have not always understood how the thanks could be so long and involved. But things look different from the inside. These acknowledgments could easily be longer than this book—the stories and people that inspired it, those whose comments and support over years helped give it shape and life—could fill volumes.

First, I thank the more than fifty children and adults of Nadomak Sunca, the real "Children's Village," of Oprtalj, Croatia, who inspired this story with theirs, and who continue to build their own bright tales. To my close companion on this writing road, Susan Van Metre, my editor, who stuck with me and the book through thick and helped thin it—with enthusiasm, interest, and keen attention to the telling of this story—a huge volume of thanks. Susan wields a mighty heart and pencil. To my son, Alex, a great storyteller in his own right, who read patiently through several drafts, watched me live among piles of paper, and has continued to make important and astoundingly insightful comments, thanks for that help and more. Thanks also to all of my friends, so ready to lend a hand or mind in any circumstance, including Steve Manes, who knows how to edit in Technicolor; Ginger de Leeuw, always amenable to figuring it out; and those willing to fall asleep with an open book and stay with the journey—Debbie McGibbon; and Craig Rennebohm and Barbara Bennett, who told me years ago of that place they had heard of: "The Children's Village." To those, wherever found, who help children and families. To the storytellers, who have known war and peace, including my grandparents, and the rest who bravely traversed lands and seas. To the many who graciously told of the lands and times of this story, particularly Sanja Barišić, who kindly read the manuscript. To all of my extended family, who so generously offer welcome, warmth, and refuge.

Since this story has been inspired by so many people and events, I know I have failed to specifically name each of those who deserve acknowledgment and thanks. To all, thank you.

ABOUT THE AUTHOR

Arthur Dorros has published more than twenty highly acclaimed picture books, including *Tonight is Carnaval, Rain Forest Secrets, Ant Cities,* and *Abuela,* which the New York Public Library named one of the "100 Picture Books Everyone Should Know." This is his first novel. He was inspired to write it after reading about the wars in the former Yugoslavia and hearing friends talk of an actual village of children—Serb, Croat, Muslim—and others living peacefully away from the conflicts that divided their country. In researching this book, Mr. Dorros traveled extensively through republics of the former Yugoslavia and stayed at "The Children's Village" in Croatia. He lives in Seattle with his family. His Web site is www.arthurdorros.com.

The text of this book is set in Charlotte Book. Typeface designer Michael Gills created the Charlotte typeface family in 1992 for the Letraset Corporation under the guidance of Colin Brignall, Art Director.

The display face used in the chapter openers is TheSans, designed by Berlin-based type designer Lucas De Groot and is part of the FF Thesis font family. FF Thesis is possibly the largest type family of all time with 144 variations.